The Hermit

A NOVEL

J.E. Jack

Dedication

To my brother Jarrod, as well as to my Aunt Colleen and Uncle Don, who without their influence in my life, the idea of this story may have never come to be. And as always, to my wife and editor, Marcel, for enhancing my life and my stories.

Table of Contents

Prologue

It was raining hard with moments of relief peppered here and there like the scattered thunderstorms that were passing through the area. It was miserable out, with the kind of wet that would soak a person to the bone if they weren't wearing rain gear. Even if they were, there was still a good chance of becoming drenched.

Nearby, there was a road cut through the forest, not far from a small village in the middle of rural America. It wasn't a busy or well-traveled road, but it was one that locals, or other random travelers, frequently used to get to and from town and other towns beyond.

An old man kept to the side, walking through the woods near the road, close enough to see the road but far enough that if a car passed, the passengers would have had to pay attention to catch sight of him. The man looked to be in his late 60s, but one couldn't really tell. He could have been younger, but his hard-living look added some years. His clothes were sturdy yet well-worn; he wasn't dirty but looked weathered. The figure cinched down the hood of his jacket to keep dry as he continued on.

In one hand he carried a walking stick, and in the other, he carried a fishing pole. It wasn't a fancy fishing pole. It was little more than a cheap, flimsy rod and reel with string attached to it. There were plenty of ponds and lakes in the area, as well as a river a few miles away, to catch food. He didn't appear to be hungry but moved with a purpose, as if it were a routine that he would have kept had it been raining, snowing or sweltering. The fact that it was raining now didn't deter him from his daily activities.

He heard a car coming from around the curve. The familiar sound of an engine and wheels roaring along the road came first and he stopped to watch as it approached. It wasn't that he didn't want to be seen, but he wasn't going to go out of his way to be noticed, either. The car came quickly out of the curve and into his sight. It was a small, blue sedan, and it was moving at a good clip. He could almost make out the driver and the other passengers in the car, but they were little more than silhouettes through the rain-beaten windshield.

As he watched, he noticed a squirrel dart out into the street in front of the car. He winced, or it may have been a squint, as he saw the furry creature come to a stop in the middle of the road, with its tail twitching. The squirrel seemed surprised to see the car come bearing in on it. It darted forward and continued for a second. The man thought it would make it across but at the last minute, the squirrel decided to change course and go back. The man could do nothing but watch as the car hit the squirrel. It never slowed down, and the squirrel became a speed bump with a resounding "thwack."

The man gave out a sigh at the disruption as the

car continued out of sight, oblivious to the wreckage it had just caused. He walked over to look at the squirrel to find that it was in its death throes, twitching wildly as the nerves inside its little body were firing their last impulses. He continued until he stood over the unfortunate, little thing and bent down to pick it up. It was still twitching in his hand as he moved back to the safety of the trees and forest. He got down on one knee and laid the creature on a bed of leaves near his foot. It had since stopped moving. He put one hand over the body and his face contorted in deep concentration. A slight glow appeared between the squirrel's body and the palm of his hand. It grew brighter and then dissipated. As quickly as the light had come, it was gone. The old man looked down at the squirrel and the squirrel looked back at him.

"Okay, you be more careful with the time you have left," the old man said before the squirrel hopped up and scampered off, leaving the old man alone again. "I'll see you again soon," he said as he got to his feet and watched the creature leave. He gave what looked like a tired smile and turned to continue his daily routine.

Chapter One

It was the last day of the school year and for brothers Chris and Brian, they were excited at the prospects that the thought of summer brought. There were four years' difference in their ages. Chris was the eldest at 15, with Brian being 11. Even though they went to different schools, they rode the same school bus home. Good ol' bus 98 with hard, green seats. During the winter, the best place to be was in the third seat from the front, where the small heater vent was located. It's amazing that whoever designed this bus thought that little heater would do anything to help. Even though it was "cool" to sit in the back, Chris always made a beeline for that seat during those cold, miserable, early mornings. Sometimes, the effort to be "cool" just wasn't worth it. But during the spring and especially now, in the afternoon on the last day of school, it was miserably hot and all the windows on the bus were open. Anything to let in the cooler air from outside helped, even if just slightly. Everyone was excited and it was noisy. The bus was full now, having just picked up the high school kids. The middle and elementary school kids were already loaded and accounted for.

Chris sat in the back with his friends. He was of average height for his age and had brown hair with blue eyes. Everyone could tell that Chris and Brian were brothers; Brian looked like a younger version of Chris, except he had green eyes.

"You gonna be around this summer?" Chris' friend Mike, asked. "My parents are putting in a pool."

"Really?" Chris asked.

"Yeah. My dad has been wanting to put one in for a while and once it's in, we are going to have a blast!" Mike said.

"Must be nice," Chris thought to himself. He knew that would never happen with his family. His mom was a single parent and even though she never let on, he knew money was tight. His mom and dad divorced years ago and with his father in the military, he wasn't around that often. Those first few years were tough with them moving around, but they had been in their current home for a couple years now, so things were a little more stable.

"I'm trying to be. I usually go to my aunt's farm for the summer, but I think I'm getting old enough to stay home," Chris said.

"Well, it'd be cool if you did. We are going to have pool parties all the time!" Mike replied.

Chris lived a couple miles away from Mike. It was only a 15-minute ride on his bicycle. He had only ridden there once, because his mom didn't like the idea of him riding so far by himself. The one time that he did go, he had to take his younger brother with him, which he wasn't really happy about, but at the same time, he felt obligated. He knew his brother couldn't stay home by himself and with his mom being busy making ends meet, he had to look out for him when she wasn't around.

There was a commotion up front, which brought his attention from the delusions of pool parties and fun times with friends, to his brother Brian. It looked like he was arguing with someone and it was getting louder.

"You take that back!" Brian yelled at another boy who was sitting in another seat closer to the front of the bus.

Chris was surprised, as Brian was usually a little more laid back. He didn't know what could have caused such a reaction. The bus was loud but then everyone quieted down to watch the scene unfold.

"No," the kid replied. He was bigger than Brian by a couple of inches. Chris only noticed this because now the other kid had gotten up and was moving closer to Brian.

"It's true and I'm not going to take it back," the kid continued.

Chris could tell that things were escalating, so he got up to intervene, but before he could, Brian attempted to punch the kid right in the nose but missed. Before the kid could respond with a punch of his own, Chris hurried forward and moved between them.

"Hey! What's this all about? Cut it out!" he said.

The kid just looked at Chris and then at Brian, "Gotta have your big brother save you, huh?"

Brian lunged again at the kid but Chris grabbed him before he could make contact.

"What's going on back there?" yelled the bus driver, looking up in the wide, overhead mirror, to see behind her.

All three–Chris, Brian and the other kid quickly yelled "nothing." Although emotions were high, no one wanted any issues on the ride home on the last day of school, right before summer vacation.

The bus driver just scowled at them in suspicion because she, too, was in a hurry to get this last ride out of the way, and went back to driving. Chris looked down at his brother, then at the other kid. The kid just harrumphed and moved back to his seat by the window to look out, ignoring them both. Everyone else on the bus, realizing the show was over, went back to whatever they were doing.

"Move over," Chris told Brian as he sat down beside him. Brian was still irritated.

"What was that about?" Chris asked.

"He said bad things about Mom and our family. It made me mad. He was also making fun of you guys in the back and I just wasn't going to have any more of it," Brian said.

Chris felt proud that Brian would stick up for himself, but he was torn because he knew that a person just can't go around hitting people they disagree with. Of course, he probably would have done the same thing, but he had to be an example, or at least try to set one.

"Brian, you shouldn't hit people."

"I know...but he just wouldn't shut up."

"How do you think Mom would feel if you got into trouble on the last day of school? You know she already has enough to deal with, right?" Chris said.

"I know," Brian quietly replied, shifting uncomfortably. "But he deserved it. He was also about to punch me, so I just went first."

"Well, who cares what he said? He's just an ignorant kid who doesn't know any better than to show he's an idiot. It's summertime. We don't have to deal with him or anyone else for the entire summer," Chris said with a smile, winking at his brother.

Brian, who had calmed down by this time, smiled back and nodded in agreement.

"Yeah–who cares?"

Instead of heading back to the rear of the bus where his friends were, Chris decided to just stay with his brother. One by one, the bus emptied as it continued its route. Mike got off before Chris and as he passed him, he told Chris to call him if he was going to stay in the area for the summer, so they could hang out.

"Sure thing," Chris said, but he wasn't confident. He knew that the chances of staying home were slim to none. Every summer, they went to stay with family up north in southern Illinois. In earlier years, it had been an issue of childcare for him and his brother, since his mom couldn't afford to pay someone to watch them while she worked. But he thought he was getting old enough that this shouldn't be an issue. He enjoyed going to the country but at the same time, he kind of wanted to stay home. Maybe just his brother could go. It would be nice to have a summer to himself, he thought. And besides, if their home near the coast of Florida was considered a small town, the rural living in southern Illinois was absolutely remote.

Chris and Brian lived near the end of the bus route, so they were always one of the earliest pick-ups and the latest drop-offs. Every day, it was close to 45 minutes on the bus to and from the different schools. Chris often thought of the families with parents who picked up their kids from school ("what luxury," Chris thought), or even the high school kids who had cars to drive to and from school. How awesome that would be but again, Chris didn't allow himself to think about such things too much, because he didn't want to dwell on hopeless situations.

When it was their turn, his brother Brian hopped up and ran off the bus without a thought in the world. As usual, Chris stopped and told Mrs. Turner, the bus driver, to have a good day and added, "and a great summer."

"Don't get into any trouble this summer and we'll see you next year," she said.

"I hope not," he thought to himself as he stepped off the last stair and heard the door close, then the engine rev behind him, as it continued on the route.

Brian ran on ahead to the front door and unlocked it, using his own key. They both had their own key, in case someone got stuck behind at school. Their home was a modular, double-wide trailer that was made to look like an actual house, with wood-grain siding and brick around the foundation. It looked like any other house on their road, except it sat a little higher. It even had a brick front porch. They didn't live in a neighborhood like most of the kids he knew. They lived on the side of a two-lane highway and there weren't any other kids their age that lived nearby.

Chris and Brian had to amuse themselves and that usually came in the form of books or some made-up game that only they would play together. They liked to go exploring in the woods across the street. It was only a small patch of trees, but that didn't stop their imaginations from making it whatever they needed it to be. That was one of the good things about heading to southern Illinois—more places to explore.

Brian turned on the TV and settled in for the afternoon cartoons. Since Chris was getting older, in the back of his mind, he thought he should be over watching cartoons, but he still enjoyed them, so settled beside Brian.

This was the schedule they had developed over the past year—they would come home, watch TV or do homework, and wait for their mom to get home. She never got home before 5 PM, so that gave the boys a couple of hours to fill the time with whatever suited them.

"Do you want to go to Aunt Christie's farm this summer?" Chris asked Brian, as they were watching TV.

Brian looked back at him like he was stupid.

"Yeah, why wouldn't I?"

"I was thinking about trying to stay here this summer," Chris said.

"That's dumb. There's nothing to do here and besides, Sam is waiting for us," Brian said.

Sam was their cousin and Aunt Christie's son. He was a couple years younger than Chris and a couple years older than Brian. Chris liked Sam just fine–in fact, he liked all the family in the country. He just wanted to do something different. Hanging out on the farm just didn't hold the same excitement that it used to. In some ways, it was similar to their home, in that there wasn't a whole lot to do, but Chris was reminded that there was more freedom to get out and about in southern Illinois. There was a small town about a mile from his aunt's farm and he did enjoy having that kind of environment where he didn't feel so constricted…but again, he just wanted something different.

"Well, I'm going to ask mom if I can stay here," Chris said.

"You are free to make dumb decisions, Chris, but you're gonna be bored. Besides, it won't be the same without you. You gotta come," Brian said. Then, remembering something, he added, "And the Darling girls, Erin and Jessica, they'll be there."

The Darling family lived a couple farms over from their aunt's farm and went to the same church in the small town nearby. They were close in age to Chris and his brother. Jessica was a year older than Chris and Erin was the same age as his brother.

"So?" Chris said.

"What? I thought you liked them," Brian said.

"I do. I mean...they are fine, but..." Chris really didn't know what to say. He did like them and enjoyed hanging out with them. In fact, he'd had a slight crush on Jessica the past couple of years, but she never showed any interest in him. She only seemed interested in older, local boys.

"But what?" Brian asked.

"It's not like they care if we show up or not."

"What are you talking about? Erin loves it when we show up...at least, I think she does," Brian scowled as he thought about it. "Well, maybe she doesn't but I sure do."

Chris didn't care. He felt that he was old enough to do his own thing this summer. He was 15 for God's sake and surely, he could stay home by himself.

The plans were always the same. Every time summer arrived, the week following the last day of school, they would pile into the car for a ten-hour ride to visit family. Their mom would stay for a couple of days before heading back, leaving Chris and Brian behind. Then a week before school started in the fall, the same routine would take place, only in reverse. Their mom would show up, stay a couple of days and then drive back home with Chris and Brian in tow. It had been this way the past several years, ever since their parents divorced and now it was just one of those things that they did.

He had told his mom that he wanted to stay home

this summer, but they hadn't had a proper conversation about it yet. With next week looming, he had to talk to his mom about it tonight. So, he waited and after a couple hours, he went out to the backyard to meet his mom when she arrived home, which would be any minute now. The property had a small parking space out front for visitors, but it also had a parking space under a metal awning that was attached over the back door. And right at 5 PM, as if on cue, he heard the familiar sound of the car arrive home. They had a gravel and shell driveway, and it made a distinctive crunching sound anytime someone walked or drove over it. He saw the small, gray sedan with his mom behind the wheel, come around the corner and park. She looked tired but smiled as she got out of the car and saw Chris waiting for her.

"How was school today?" she asked.

"It was fine...kind of hard to have a bad last day of school," Chris said.

"Thank God it's Friday, right?" she said.

He wanted to get right into the business of summer plans but since he could plainly see she was tired, he decided to wait until later, after she had some time to wind down from her day at work.

"How was work?" Chris asked.

"Didn't I say, 'Thank God it's Friday?'" she replied, as if that should be all the explanation he needed for an answer.

"That bad?"

"No, it was okay. It's just been a long week. The

orders were behind, so I had to catch up. Just tedious," she said.

Chris didn't know exactly what she did. He only knew that she worked at a warehouse in an administrative department and had to deal with orders and vendors. She had worked there for a while and it paid the bills.

Later that evening and while they were having dinner, Chris decided that it was as good a time as any to bring up the subject of staying home for the summer.

"Mom, can I stay home this summer?"

Brian was at the table and just muttered to himself, "That's stupid."

Chris ignored him while he waited for his mom to answer.

"Who will watch after Brian if you are here?" she asked.

This caused a reaction in both Brian and Chris, with Brian blurting out, "I don't need him to 'watch' me."

Chris was about to say the same thing but added, "Well, he is going to be hanging out with Sam, so he won't be alone."

"Sam is a little young. I think Christie likes having you around when you all are running around the woods. It makes her feel better that you are all together–you know– safety in numbers."

"Mom, I don't want to go," Chris said.

"What would you do here all summer?" she asked.

"I don't know but I just want to do something different. Mike said his parents are putting in a pool this summer," Chris said.

"Chris, I know you don't really want to go this summer. You've been hinting at it for the past few weeks. I'm not dumb," she said.

"Then, can I?" Chris asked.

"Listen, would you please go this summer…one last time? Next summer, I promise, you can stay home. You will be old enough to drive but this summer, I just don't want you staying at the house by yourself. It's not healthy, and I don't want to have to worry about you while I'm at work," she said.

Chris was frustrated. He knew his mom was tired and needed a break, but he also wanted a little independence. "But mom…" he began.

His mom just looked at him with finality and said, "Chris, I need you to go."

He wanted to argue but he knew from experience what that look meant, and once he saw it, there was no changing her mind. In the back of his mind, he couldn't help but wonder what he would do here all summer, anyway. They didn't live close to anything and daytime TV sucked, with all game shows or soap operas. It wasn't that he really didn't want to go to the country; it was just that he wanted to do something different–anything different. But his mom was right. He did have to watch Brian, regardless of how Brian felt about it. He felt responsible for his brother. What if something were to happen this summer and he wasn't there? He also thought about Jessica, the girl that lived down the lane from his aunt's farm. Maybe he could talk to her more this summer...if she wasn't too busy.

"Okay. Fine..." he said.

"Don't worry, Chris. You and Brian are going to have a great time this summer."

"Heck yeah, we are," Brian agreed.

With Chris now resigned to the fact that he was going and there were no other options available, he responded in the only way he thought to. He looked at both Brian and his mother and grumbled, "I doubt it."

Chapter Two

The next day, they packed everything they would need for the summer. For Chris and Brian, that included two suitcases each for clothes and whatever else they wanted to bring. Brian was obsessed with the military, so he took his toy guns along. Besides his clothes, Chris took some books; they were from one of his favorite fantasy series and he hadn't had a chance to read them yet. It was a long ride to get to his aunt's farm and he looked forward to passing the time deep in the mountain mists of Ildoran, the mystical land the books were set in. His brother saw his books and decided to bring along some comic books. Their mom only brought one small suitcase–enough for a couple of days, as she would be coming back shortly.

They piled into the family car and left the town and the summer of Mike's pool parties behind. As they got on the highway, Chris thought to himself, "Well, maybe there'll be time to go to Mike's house to enjoy the pool after summer ends." The way to southern Illinois was quite familiar to them all. In fact, even though Chris had just gotten his learner's permit, he could have driven all the way to his aunt's farm with his eyes closed. They had come this way so often; they didn't even need to look at the maps anymore. Chris still enjoyed thumbing through the various maps, though; he often thought of the names of towns that he saw printed on the pages and imagined what all those places might be like. He was naturally curious about all of it. How did those towns get their names? Who lived there? What stories were being told that he was missing by not living there? In the end, even if they knew where they were going, it's always a good idea to have a map in the event that they lost their way or had to figure out a different route. This is why his mom bought the latest edition of the 1994 Rand McNally Road Atlas the week before they left. It had a picture of a mountain on the front cover and on the inside were the colorful maps that Chris couldn't resist.

They also had the obligatory road trip snacks and soft drinks in an ice chest. Brian was crazy about Capri Suns, so they had a few in there, just for him. Chris couldn't help but feel that spark of excitement that comes with being on a road trip. Even if they were going to the same place that they went every year, it was still an adventure to get there.

About an hour after they started, Brian was already asleep in the back seat. Chris kind of envied him, but he got a full night's rest and was wide awake. He looked at his mom, who was just humming along to the music and watching the road.

"Do you think you will want me to drive?" Chris asked.

"Oh, no," his mom replied. "I know you just got your learner's permit, but I don't really feel comfortable to let you drive on the interstate yet."

"But we aren't going to be on the interstate for another hour."

His mom thought about it and then agreed, "Okay. Next stop, we will switch."

A few miles later found them pulling off into a gas station and since they had just started the journey north an hour before, no one needed to use the restroom. Chris and his mom switched positions and now his brother was alert and awake because Chris driving was a big deal. His life was in his brother's hands if he screwed it up. Chris, however, wasn't thinking along these lines. He was excited but nervous, for sure. He'd only had his permit to drive for a couple months. It was the first time he'd been allowed to drive on an actual road and not some neighborhood or parking lot. He adjusted the seat and mirrors, just like they had taught him in driver's ed. The class was great, but it didn't really get into driving beyond the school parking lot. So much for that experience.

His mom took a deep breath and said, "Okay, let's go. Brian, put on your seatbelt!"

Brian did so and Chris put the car into drive. They started forward and as they left the parking lot, Chris didn't see the large rock on the passenger side as he turned. The rock didn't fit so well under the front wheel, causing them to jolt to a stop. Chris didn't know what to do, so he stepped on the gas and immediately had a sinking feeling as he felt the car go over the rock and heard the unmistakable sound of grating as the rock dragged along on the right underside of the car. After he cleared the obstacle, his mom yelled, "Stop!"

She got out and looked at the damage. From Chris' viewpoint, he could tell his mom was not happy. He got out to inspect the damage, as well, and could hear another unmistakable sound–the sound of air whooshing out of the right, front tire. By this point, Brian had gotten out, as well.

"Wow, Chris–you really messed up this time," he said.

"Shut up," Chris replied.

He felt horrible. His mom just looked at the car with an unreadable look on her face, but it was certainly not a happy one. "I'm sorry, mom. I didn't see it."

She sighed and then replied, "It's okay, son. Let's go ahead and change the tire. We still have a long way to go."

They went to the trunk and removed the luggage; Chris took the spare tire out from below the carpet liner, along with the jack that came with a car. Thankfully, the car had a full-sized spare tire. It was already warm out and the sweat began beading across Chris' forehead as he started winching the jack to lift the car. His mom helped when it came to taking the punctured tire off and getting the other in place. Fifteen minutes later, they had packed everything back into the trunk and were ready to go again. Feeling dejected, Chris returned to sit in the passenger seat. They didn't talk much, as Chris felt horrible and had nothing to say, and neither did anyone else. The weight of what just happened grew in Chris' mind, and though his mom never complained about money in front of them, he knew paying for a new tire was something they just didn't need right now.

"Mom, I can see if I can use Aunt Christie's lawn mower and mow some yards in the town nearby, so I will pay for a new tire," Chris finally said after a while.

"Honey, it's okay. The hole in the tire didn't look that big. We'll get it patched when we get there," his mom said.

The bubble of unease popped, and everything was back to normal again. Though Chris would be embarrassed about the moment for months to come.

"So, what are you both wanting to do when you get there?" his mom asked, making conversation.

Brian jumped right in with his plans. "Oh I'm gonna go over to Gopher's gully and see how the fort is. Then at some point, I'm gonna walk over to town. And I'm sure at some point I'll visit all the other cousins..." He continued on but Chris was lost in his thoughts. Just what was it that he wanted to do this summer?

Gopher's gully was an area on his aunt's farm where, last summer, they had constructed a small fort out of logs and tree limbs. It was also last summer that he, Brian, Sam and Uncle Bob built a raft out of few logs to test out on one of the many ponds on the farm. Unfortunately, shortly after launching, the raft promptly sank to the bottom in a deep part of the pond. Brian had gone under with it and his pants leg and foot got caught up in it. If it hadn't been for Sam being close by and thinking quickly to help Brian get untangled, who knew what could have happened? At any rate, it all turned out okay, but disappointing that all that work they put into building the raft was so quickly undone when it sank. It was kind of funny to think about his brother spluttering in the water, saying he was fine…that is, of course, only after they had determined that he was, in fact, fine. Uncle Bob was Aunt Christie's husband and Sam's father, and he often helped the boys tinker and build things when they all got together. Chris wasn't yet sure what projects he wanted to work on this summer.

Brian was still going on about what he wanted to do. Chris thought about the summer before last and another memory boiled up. They had acquired an old go-cart, so had created a racetrack of sorts in one of the fields. However, the ground was so uneven, the engine ended up breaking apart from trying to drive it on such rough terrain; it never ran again. One could only walk to the nearby town so much, especially in the heat of the summer. Looking down at the book in his hand, he hoped that maybe while visiting some of the other relatives in the area, he could go to the library or secondhand bookstore and pick up more books. Eventually, his brother stopped talking and his mom turned the conversation toward him.

"And you? What do you have plans for?" she asked.

"I'm not sure. Maybe go fishing. Maybe go explore in the woods. I don't know. I mean…come on, mom—it's not like there is much to do," he said.

"Well, I am sure something will come up," she

responded.

Chris turned his attention to his book and was soon lost in the fantasy adventure. In the back of his mind, he always wanted something interesting or magical to happen to him, but things like that never happen in real life, at least not to him.

The hours, as well as the miles, passed by. State lines became progress points with each one causing more excitement to build, because that meant they were getting closer to their destination. They crossed the last progress point as they came over the bridge that spanned the Ohio River between Kentucky and Illinois, the welcome sign letting them know that they were finally in the Land of Lincoln. Even Brian, who was slumped in the back seat, got up for the occasion. Chris looked up and noticed, then went back to reading. They still had almost an hour to go before they would arrive to Aunt Christie's. As they eventually got closer, and turned off onto Route 45, Chris put his book to the side because things were now becoming familiar.

He had noticed it before, but he was reminded every time he came up here to southern Illinois from Florida, that the trees were different than the ones from home. Tall, straight pines gave way to oak, maple, elm, sycamore and other more interesting trees. Although there were some of the same trees that were in Florida, they didn't have the same abundance as they had in southern Illinois. Leaves as big as your outstretched hand were quite different from pine needles and cones. Chris wondered if people that lived here would notice that difference heading to the coast of Florida.

They passed small communities, homes, and farms. The rolling hills of varying shades of green were beautiful, not to mention the added dots of farm animals that graced the view. It was all so very picturesque. Some of Chris' earliest memories were of riding in the bed of his aunt and uncle's truck with these views and even at a very young age, the sense of wonder struck deep. There was nothing better than driving, or riding in Chris' case, through these roads that had stories to tell, if one was willing to listen to them.

After about forty minutes of riding on the two-lane highway, they passed by a couple of villages that may have been inhabited by two to three hundred souls (at most) and were named after Civil War generals or forts. They came to yet another village of Stonemill, that, like many others on this road, was just a dot of life in the hustle and bustle of the world. This one, however, Chris and Brian knew well. It was the little village that was only about a mile from Aunt Christie's house. It had been named after a stone mill that serviced the area a hundred years or more in the past, but the history had been sketchy; no one was certain where the location of the actual mill had been.

The excitement in the car built as the finish line was just a few minutes away and their journey would come to an end. Chris became aware of his legs cramping and thought about how wonderful it would feel to get out and stretch. They turned off onto an even smaller road that passed through Stonemill, which took them out into the country. About a mile from the village, they turned onto a lane that would take them to their final destination. It was a large, two-story house with light blue siding and white trim, which overlooked the sweeping valley to the front. Chris had forgotten how beautiful the view was. It seemed as if he always forgot, then every summer, he was again reminded when he returned.

It was late afternoon, almost evening, when they pulled into the driveway. The front door opened, as if someone had been waiting for them and indeed there had been. Sam came bounding out from the house and ran across the yard to meet them as Chris' mom turned off the car. Sam was a light blond, almost white-haired, skinny kid who was tall for his age; he was taller than Brian, for sure, but not quite as tall as Chris yet. It was safe to assume, though, that in a few years, he would tower over both of them. Aunt Christie came out of the house, followed by Uncle Bob. Aunt Christie had a welcoming demeanor, as usual. She had dark brown, curly hair that she kept short. Uncle Bob had a serious look to him that would be off-putting to those that didn't know him. Once you did get to know him, though, you knew he was the kind of guy that you could count on in almost any situation.

As they got out of the car, Sam pelted them with questions about their trip, not even waiting for an answer before going to the next one in his excitement. Chris and Brian lived in a town and although they didn't live in a suburb or neighborhood that had a lot of kids, they had each other. They didn't live in the country on a farm like Sam did, so Chris was sure that he got lonely through the year, waiting for them to visit every summer.

"How was the trip?" Aunt Christie asked.

"Oh…it was a trip," Chris' mom replied, then continued, "It wasn't bad once we got going. We did have a bit of a hiccup starting out."

Chris' face turned a shade of red but he kept quiet as he retrieved the luggage from the trunk. Brian giggled beside Chris, noticing Chris' new color. "Shut up," Chris said.

"I didn't say anything," Brian replied.

"I know, but you were thinking about it," Chris said.

"Maybe…" Brian said.

Sam came to the trunk and grabbed some of the luggage to help bring it inside. It took the focus off of the conversation that the grownups were having and changed the topic.

"Did you bring your toy guns?" Sam asked.

"Sure did. They are in that duffel bag," Brian replied, pointing at the bag that Sam had in his hand.

"Awesome. We will go attack Rock Ridge at first light," Sam said.

"Roger," Brian replied, dropping into what they thought military lingo would sound like.

Every summer, this was a big and recurring activity of theirs–pretending that they were in the military, on patrol in the woods around the farm.

Rock Ridge was a ridge in one of the hills halfway between the farm and Stonemill. They found it a couple years back; it had large rocks, or boulders out in the middle of nowhere, near the top of a rather large hill. Chris was getting older, but even he still liked to participate in these "patrols."

"Are you hungry?" his aunt asked them all.

"Sure am!" Brian said.

"Well, let's go inside, out of this heat, and fix something to eat," she replied.

They obliged and headed into the house. Chris and Brian went ahead and took their luggage upstairs to Sam's room. It was a rather large bedroom and had more than enough room for three boys to stay in quite comfortably. They also had a spare bedroom downstairs that Chris and Brian's mom used when she visited. There were plenty of options because they had quite a bit of family in the area, but they usually stayed with Aunt Christie.

"So, Sam…how are Erin and Jessica doing?" Brian asked.

"Fine, I guess. I don't see them too often, except at church," Sam replied. "Why do you ask?"

"Oh, I don't know. I was just curious," Brian said, getting a little uneasy.

Sam, sensing his unease, smiled like a shark and went in for the kill. "Oh, I see…You gotta crush on Erin, don't you?"

"No. No, I don't," Brian said, then quipped, "I just

like her company better than I do yours."

"That was quick," Chris said.

Turning toward his brother, Brian said, "Hey, I can be surprising at times."

They returned downstairs to Aunt Christie standing over the stove, cooking something that smelled fantastic. Chris and Brian's mom was sitting at the kitchen table. They were laughing like children. This always happened when they got together. Chris enjoyed listening to them reminisce with old stories and laugh whenever they all had the chance to hang out together; it was infectious. It was so refreshing to see his mom enjoy the time with her sister.

"You boys get settled?" Aunt Christie asked.

"Yes Ma'am," replied Chris.

"Okay, good."

Dinner was ready shortly after and it was burgers; burgers made with love were far better than any fast-food burgers. Chris had two and they tasted great after being in a car all day. He was stuffed but kept eating, as he just couldn't help himself. Slowly, he made his way from the kitchen table into the living room. The conversation continued and Chris just listened in. Brian and Sam disappeared into the house, probably back up to Sam's room, he thought. Now that he was here, he was glad to be there. He had really just wanted to do something different, but then being surrounded by familiarity was comforting and he had always enjoyed it here. In fact, in that moment, he couldn't figure out why he hadn't wanted to come.

Uncle Bob was watching TV but it was coming in and out; they only received three or four channels. It was fuzzy and whenever there was a strong gust of wind that hit the antenna outside, it would mess up the picture for a little bit. They also didn't run the air conditioner, which made it a bit stifling at times, but they had a huge attic fan that cooled down the house surprisingly well. It was interesting and honestly a little counterintuitive to Chris, but with the fan blowing outside, it created a draft inside the house so there was a constant breeze coming through the open windows. In fact, now that he was thinking about it, he could hear the fan, but it was one of those things that after a while, you just tuned it out.

It wasn't long before Chris' eyes began to get droopy and he yawned. Yep, it was time for bed, Chris thought to himself. After the long day of travel, he was certainly ready. He said "good night" to his Mom and aunt, then trudged upstairs. Sam and Brian were already in the room, talking, when he came in.

"Yeah, he keeps to himself, I've only seen a glimpse of him once," Chris heard Sam saying as he shut the door behind him.

"Really? That's so interesting," Brian said.

"What are you two talking about?" Chris asked.

"Oh, Sam was telling me about a hermit who lives in the woods," Brian answered.

"What? There's a hermit? Where at?" Chris asked, interest piqued.

"Yeah," Sam said. "Along the road to town, he

lives up on the one of the hills near Rock Ridge. He came and asked my dad if he could fish in one of the ponds on our land. I guess he saw all the 'no trespassing' signs and didn't want to cause trouble."

"Your dad let him?" Chris asked.

"Yeah, he doesn't mind people using the land if they ask. It's only when they don't ask that he gets mad," Sam said.

Chris remembered one incident a couple years back when there were a couple of hunters on the farm without permission, and sure enough–he hadn't ever seen Uncle Bob that angry. It was a big misunderstanding and the hunters apologized but he certainly didn't want to be on the wrong end of his uncle's wrath.

"How long has he been around? And you said you've seen him?" Chris asked.

"I'm not sure how long he's been around. I heard that he's been around a while and at first, no one ever saw him but lately, he's being seen more and more...obviously, he is a hermit," Sam said with a laugh at something he thought was funny, but no one else did. When he saw that his humor wasn't shared, he continued, "Anyway...like I said, I saw a glimpse of him the other day while we were heading to town. He was out at the pond where we always go fishing. I mentioned it to dad and all he said was to leave him alone and don't bother him."

"Huh. Weird." Chris said, to which they all agreed.

"Who wants to be a hermit?" Chris thought to himself, although the idea of one nearby intrigued him. Why would someone give up the comforts of life and leave it all behind? He probably has some secrets. Maybe he was a mass murderer that changed his ways...or perhaps, he was mentally unstable. Who knew? The subject quickly changed to other, very important things like, which comic books were currently their favorite and other topics that weren't very important in the grand scheme of things, but in the minds of young teenagers, were. Unless, of course, it was the topic of girls, which was always important! But even so, the conversation eventually died down and everyone prepared for bed. As Chris lay in his bed, which was one of the fold-away type beds that weren't comfortable beyond twenty minutes, he noticed they must have changed out the mattress, because it was a little better than what he remembered. Brian had a spot on a couch that was in the same room and Sam was in his own bed. They continued to talk in the dark, but Chris' eyelids were getting heavier and heavier, so he began to drift off. Before he was fully asleep, he had one last thought: he wondered if he would see the hermit this summer.

Chapter Three

Chris woke up to the smell of breakfast that obviously included bacon. It was a glorious smell to wake up to. He hoped Aunt Christie made those homemade, buttermilk biscuits that he loved so much. Every time she made them, she complained about how they came out, but they were always delicious. Chris thought it was her way of under-selling and over-performing, but whatever...he loved them each and every time.

He quickly got up and headed downstairs. Brian and Sam were already downstairs, sitting at the dining table. Sam turned toward Brian and said "I love it when you guys visit. My mom pulls out all stops when it comes to making food for you."

Chris took his seat. Most of the food was already on the table and his mouth started to water, looking at the crispy bacon, scrambled eggs and there it was–white sausage gravy. This meant his favorite component of this delectable breakfast, the buttermilk biscuits, were on their way. The rest of the family came into the dining room and took their seats. Aunt Christie came in last, bringing the pan that held the warm biscuits.

"Oh, these biscuits aren't going to be any good. The humidity was just too high today, and they didn't form correctly."

Chris just smiled at himself. They were always good...hot with the right amount of crisp on the outside and fluff on the inside. Another thing that never failed is that he always felt miserable afterwards because he stuffed himself. But, it was a small price to pay for the goodness of it all. They said grace and dug right in.

The conversation went as anyone expected. "Would you pass the gravy? How did you sleep last night? Would you like some juice...or milk?"

It didn't take long for the food to clear. There were rarely leftovers and if there were, they never stuck around long. His uncle Bob did what he always did at the very end of breakfast; he'd pour sorghum syrup on his plate, then take a knife and cut butter off from the stick, then mix them together. He would then grab a biscuit to continue the beauty of a well-made and homemade, from "scratch" breakfast.

When breakfast was over, Chris was ready for a nap. The food was great, but it always left him tired. They had to get ready for church, though, so he quickly took a shower and got out the iron to make sure his clothes didn't look like he had just pulled them out from a suitcase...which he had. He got dressed and was ready in no time. Everyone else went through the motions and were ready to go. During the summer, anytime the church doors were open, they would be there in attendance, starting Sunday mornings with Sunday School, then to Sunday worship, and even Wednesday nights. But on the weekends when Chris' mom visited, they would skip

Sunday school.

Church started promptly at 11 AM and they found themselves in their hard, wooden pews at five minutes before the start of the service. Chris looked around the sanctuary of the small church as people from the local community filed in from outside. It was a small church, with a congregation consisting of 80 people on the best of days but on most days, it was a good and normal-sized crowd at around 30. A few folks from the community who had come to know Brian and Chris over the years, welcomed them back for the summer.

There was a rope in the foyer where, each week, one lucky kid was allowed to ring the bell to let the habitants of Stonemill know that church was in session. Chris had done it a few times in summers past. He could still remember the feel of the rope as the bell shifted the weight of the pull. Sure enough, it still brought delight to the kids, as evidenced by today's honorary bell-ringer almost being lifted off his feet as he held on to the rope.

At the last minute, he saw Erin and Jessica come in with their family and take seats in their normal place. They saw Brian and Chris and both groups waved to each other in greeting. Chris thought that they still looked cute; he looked forward to saying "Hello" as there would be time to talk afterwards.

Church started soon thereafter and some of the members from the congregation shuffled to the pews behind the pulpit to form the makeshift choir. The church only had one piano off to the left of the small platform where the pastor's wife, Mrs. Williams, took a seat and led the worship part of the service. She called out different songs and page numbers where it could be found in the hymnals. Like with most smaller churches, the hymnals were thick, hardbound books that were handily placed in slots on the back of the pews so people sitting in the pew behind had access to them.

The worship ended in a prayer, after which the offering plate was passed around, which was another special treat for the kids that were allowed to participate in the weekly ritual. Kids (or different adult members, if there weren't enough kids present), would stand at the ends of the rows and send the collection plate in an orderly fashion through the rows of the church. This never took long, as it was quite a small church with only nine or so rows of pews on each side of the main aisle.

Mr. Williams, the preacher, a skinny man behind glasses and with a loud voice, got up behind the pulpit and started to preach. The whole thing was a familiar experience to Chris, who by now, had come to view this as a routine since he'd been coming here every summer for several years. The preacher started off with a story and then added a bit of scripture, almost like a chef adds ingredients in such a way that makes the end product that much more satisfying. A little salt, a pinch of pepper, a touch of thyme; gradually let simmer, then evolve into a boil. It was much the same with the small village preacher building to a crescendo as his voice got louder and louder, complete with "Jee-sus" and pronouncing other words in similar affect.

The service came to an end an hour later, wrapping up with an alter call and final prayer. The congregation filed out in similar fashion as to how they had filed in–with those that wanted to gossip sticking around to chat, and those that wanted to go home making a beeline for their cars parked in the gravel parking lot across the street.

Brian and Sam headed over to talk to Erin and since he didn't really have anything better to do, Chris decided to go say "Hello" to Jessica. Erin and Jessica were definitely sisters; being only a few years apart in age, they looked almost the same. They both had long, dark brown hair with subtle curls, and fair skin. Erin was on the verge of being gangly, heading into the early teenage years, but Jessica was heading out of the gangly stage into the young woman stage. In fact, to Chris, Jessica had changed a lot since he saw her last. She wasn't wearing the glasses he was used to seeing on her and she was...wearing makeup! It wasn't in an overly flashy, heavy way that some girls at that age thought looked best, but in a light, almost imperceptible way that only highlighted her natural beauty. He hadn't noticed from across the sanctuary but as he got closer, he thought to himself, "Holy crap! She is really pretty!"

Brian and Sam were excited as they talked with Erin about plans for the summer and stories from the past year. Brian filled her in on what had happened to him since last summer, and he listened to her as she did the same. Jessica was to the side, waiting for her sister, so they could leave and go home. Their parents were already outside.

"Hey Jessica. How are you?" Chris managed. His tongue seemed to be working against him since he noticed that she was pretty.

"I'm doing okay. How have you been?" She smiled.

"Well, I'm back here for another summer," Chris said.

"I'm sorry," she quickly replied, then snickered.

"It's not that bad. I actually like it here."

Of course, he kept the fact that he had wanted to stay in Florida this summer to himself. But it wasn't a total lie, as the truth was that he really did like it here. Sure, it was a slower pace than even his small town back home, but it was also magical in a way.

"I don't know why you do; I can't wait to get out of here," she said, then looking at her watch, she frowned.

"Come on, Erin. We have to go. I need to go call Brandon," Jessica said to her sister.

"Okay," Erin replied to Jessica with a scowl, and then turned toward Brian and Sam. "She has to go call her boyfriend. Ugh...well, if you get a chance, come down to our house sometime while you are here."

The boys agreed and then all three of them followed the girls outside. The girls got into the car where their parents were waiting and left. Sam's parents were already in their truck, as well, and started it when they arrived. All three of the boys jumped into the truck bed and settled down for the short ride home. Chris always enjoyed riding in the bed of the truck–the wind in his hair, the freshness of the air flowing over his face as he looked out over the farmland, unimpeded by the vehicle window or frame. He imagined this would be how flying would feel, if one could actually fly. He also liked riding in the bed of the truck at night, in the country; the night sky looked quite different than the night sky did in the town he lived in. Here, with little to no artificial light, one could see billions of stars but at home, one could see only the very brightest of stars, with the light pollution masking the darkness of night.

They arrived back to the house shortly after noon. The heat of the day was rising off the road in the distance in waves, which only added to the feeling that it was hotter than it actually was. They spent the rest of the day inside and time went by slowly, yet also quickly in the way that Chris imagines it does for everyone.

They went back to church that evening and it was pretty much the same experience as before, but with a smaller crowd. The next morning, it was time for Chris and Brian's mom to return home and leave them behind for a couple of months. She took Chris to the side. "Chris, I'm counting on you to take care of Brian this summer. Make sure to keep an eye on him," she said.

"Of course. I mean...he is old enough to take care of himself, but I'll keep an eye on him as I throw him to the wolves," he joked.

"I'm not kidding. Keep your eye on him and mind your aunt this summer," she said.

"Okay. I will," he replied, thinking to himself, "When have I ever not done those things?"

She went over to Brian and said something to a similar effect. Brian nodded and said "Yes, ma'am." His mom then went over and talked to Aunt Christie while Chris and Brian took her luggage and packed it into her trunk. It was time for her to leave and she gave them a big hug.

"Love you!" she said.

"Love you too, mom," they both replied.

"Call us when you get home to let us know that you made it safely. It doesn't matter how late," Aunt Christie told her.

"I will."

She then got in the car and waved as she backed out of the driveway and started down the lane, with Brian running behind her and stopping at the road. They waved until they could no longer see her.

Brian turned around and said to Chris, "Let the summer begin!"

Chapter Four

Monday morning came, and the boys decided it would be best to go fishing early, as that was the best time to catch fish. Dawn and dusk always seemed to yield the best results.

Sam loved fishing. For Chris and Brian, it was just an activity to pass the time. They enjoyed the experience and skill it took to catch fish but once they did, they would throw the fish back, as they didn't really like the taste of it. But it was pretty exciting waiting with anticipation of the strike, hooking and then reeling the fish in as it struggled to escape.

They left the house armed with fishing poles, tackle boxes and backpacks that held their lunch if they decided to stay out all day and became hungry. They started down the road toward the pond, which was about a quarter of a mile away. It would have been a shorter route had they gone cross country over the farmland but with the overgrowth, it was faster to walk there by road. The pond was right off the road and had views of its own of the valley that the farm overlooked. The sun was just beginning its ascent of the day and was well within the "golden hour," an hour after sunrise or an hour before sunset, during which the sun cast a golden hue upon everything. It was absolutely beautiful. As Chris looked over the farmland, he saw the hills, the fields and the large bales of hay, all of which created a very picturesque scene. They hopped the fence from the road and walked just a little farther to reach the pond. The pond wasn't very large, but was too deep for the cows to wade in to cool off. It took maybe five minutes to walk around the whole pond, if that. The water was still and there were small tendrils of steam rising off the surface, which would disappear shortly with the continued rising of the sun.

When they arrived, they noticed they weren't alone at the pond. There was a lone figure on the far side, who had also noticed their arrival. "That's the hermit," Sam whispered loudly to Brian and Chris.

Chris, being the oldest, felt immediately responsible and wasn't sure what to expect since he hadn't expected to see anyone else here. They never had before. The hermit raised his hand in a wave and then went back to fishing on his side. The boys returned the wave.

"Stay near me," Chris said.

"That's fine with me," Brian said.

"Well, my dad said he could be here, so he probably isn't too bad," Sam said.

"I don't care. We don't know him," Chris replied. "Stay near me."

They stayed on their side and began to fish. There was a bit of tension in the air, since now, they had to share a location with someone they didn't know and had never had to do that before. What was once a

44

carefree experience, where they felt comfortable to say anything or yell in excitement to one another, they were rather subdued this morning, due to this newcomer.

Chris looked across the pond at the hermit. The hermit looked worn but clean. His clothes had the same quality–worn but clean. The view of this man didn't match Chris' impression of what he thought a hermit would look like. For some reason, when he thought of a hermit, he thought of a character from one of his favorite fantasy novels who couldn't let go of his precious ring and lived on an island in the middle of an underground lake. Obviously, this person was nothing like what he had thought. The hermit across the pond noticed him looking at him and nodded. Surprised, Chris nodded back and then went back to fishing. And that's the way the morning went. The hermit stayed on his side and the boys stayed on theirs. The fish weren't biting...at least not for them. The hermit, however, seemed to catch a fish every few minutes. He didn't throw them back.

After about an hour or so, the boys' boredom grew, with the lack of fish biting and the fact that an interloper had intruded on their peaceful morning, simply by his presence.

"Do you guys want to walk to town?" Brian asked, referring to Stonemill. It was hardly a town (heck, it was barely a village), but it did have a bank, a post office, and a filling station that was on its last leg, as well as a small, country grocery store. It wasn't a large store; it had maybe a few aisles of different canned goods and a deli counter where locals could watch as the deli worker sliced the limited variety of meats and cheeses. The boys liked to walk to the store and grab a bottled coke or other soft drink. Something about drinking a cold soda from a hard glass bottle just seemed to taste better.

"Sure, let's stash our fishing gear somewhere and we can pick it up on the way back," Chris said.

"What if the hermit finds it? He might take it," Brian said.

"We can walk up a ways and throw it in some bushes," Sam said.

They packed up their things and made their way back to the road. They waved at the hermit as they left, and he waved back. No sense in not being cordial. They walked a little way down the road, toward town, and found a suitable spot that wouldn't be seen from the road, then ditched their stuff there. Without anything in their hands weighing them down, they then headed toward town.

Halfway toward town, there was a small community cemetery called Bliss-Deaton. It was named after two original family names that had settled in the area before Stonemill was a town. Every time they walked by, the boys would make a detour through the graveyard. The gravel road that went around the perimeter of the burial ground was almost overgrown with grass. For whatever reason, it fascinated the boys to peruse the headstones and read the names of people and the dates they had lived. They didn't know any of them, but some headstones they recognized on sight, due to their many visits over the years.

They slowly walked through and read the names of the departed. One stuck out to Chris; it was the grave of a girl named Mary Teller who had been murdered fourteen years ago, in 1980, at the tender age of fourteen. It was a big story in the area at the time. Apparently, someone had killed her in a town on the other side of the county but she wasn't found until a couple years ago, before being buried here shortly after. "How sad," he thought to himself. She never got a real chance to live. But cemeteries did that to him—they always left him with a sense of life, death, and somberness, which was a lot to think about for a fifteen-year-old. They quickly forgot about the cemetery and its inhabitants as they headed on their way.

"So where do you think that hermit came from?" Brian asked.

"I have no idea," Sam replied.

"Really? No one has any idea?" Chris asked.

"No. He was just here one day, not long ago, just after winter," Sam said.

"Weird. I wonder what his story is," Chris said.

"Yeah. He isn't what I pictured a hermit as," Sam said.

"What did you picture him as?" Brian asked.

"Oh, I don't know…I was thinking of the Gollum character from that one book," Sam said.

"Ha! I thought the same," Chris said.

"Y'all are stupid. Gollum was a creature, and he isn't even real," Brian said.

"Oh yeah? What did you picture him as when you heard the word 'hermit?'" Chris asked.

"I don't know…some old guy in the woods?" Brian stated questionably, but then continued, "I know one thing though–I'd love to have that invisible ring so I could disappear from you guys," Brian said.

"I wish you had one, too," Sam said, smiling. They all laughed at this and continued walking. A few minutes later had them entering Stonemill, and after a few blocks, they arrived at the small goods store in the center of town, right off of Route 45. They opened the screen door and walked in. The spring on the door smacked the door closed after them. A middle-aged woman, Mrs. Willing, was behind the store counter and greeted them as they came in. She looked worn out, red-faced and sweaty. She also looked like she had plenty of places she would have rather been than behind the counter there, but at least she was nice and greeted them. Mrs. Willing had worked there for as long as the boys could remember. She lived about a block away and didn't have a car, so she walked to and from work. The boys greeted her back. It was a bit stifling in the store, with overhead fans moving hot air around, which would only get worse as the day wore on.

"Sorry. The AC is busted," Mrs. Willing said.

After a few seconds, Chris commiserated with her desire to be anywhere other than inside the store. They quickly picked out some drinks and paid for them at the counter. Beads of sweat were already forming across their faces. They hurriedly left the building to get back out into the breeze. Sure, it was hot outside, but not nearly as bad as it was inside.

Stonemill, as mentioned before, was a small village. It consisted of six cross streets and no traffic lights. It was doing well enough just to have stop signs. Right through the middle of town ran Route 45, which connected Mobile, Alabama all the way to Ontonagon, Michigan, with many stops like Stonemill along the way. It also had two country roads that led to other towns farther away, one of those roads being the one they walked into town on. Chris always thought it was weird that Mobile, Alabama wasn't very far from where he lived in Florida, yet it seemed so far from here. It was strange that two different communities with people he knew could go about life without thought of one another, even though one common road connected them.

"Well, now what?" Brian said as he sipped on his drink from the bottle.

"I wish we had some bicycles for all of us. We could really go far, maybe even to the next town over," Sam said.

The next town over was a bit bigger. It had a full-blown grocery store and a pool hall that Sam was thinking about. The pool hall had some arcade games and several billiard tables, but it was at least six miles away. Sam had only seen it in passing when he went into town to the grocery store with his parents. He was never allowed to go in because 1) his parents were always in a hurry to get the shopping done and

2) the place was filled with cigarette smoke, as it was primarily for people older than him. He had really wanted to go check it out, though. It simply fascinated him.

"Yeah, but that's a distance. We'd be taking a shower in sweat halfway there," Chris said.

"We could go over and sit in the Catholic church for a little bit. They are always open and thankfully, they always have the air conditioner on," Sam said.

The Catholic church was on the way home, so it made sense to take advantage of a few moments of coolness before heading back to the farm. To Chris, the whole thought of Catholicism was foreign to him, as his whole family had been raised Protestant all their lives, Southern Baptist to be specific. But the few times he had run into Father Bishop the past couple of years, he'd always been nice to them, even if they were heretics.

"Sure. That sounds like a good idea," Chris said.

They finished their drinks on the front sidewalk of the store, then headed back inside to cash in their bottles. They got five cents for every empty bottle that they turned in and for kids on a limited budget, anything helped. The lady behind the counter gave them each a nickel and they were out the door again, with the screen door slamming behind them.

"Sorry!" Brian yelled back through the screen door. They heard a muffled, "It's all right," reply. The boys walked three blocks over to the Catholic church and sure enough, the front door was unlocked. They went in and were met with the immediate coolness of an air conditioned inside. There was no one else around and it had the feeling of an old library, noticeably quiet and sacred. Even though Chris didn't grow up Catholic, he always thought their churches were very pretty, even this one with a small congregation had beautiful stained glass windows that glowed as the sunlight beamed through them. It gave them an almost neon glow. Everything was so ornate; it was very different from the Baptist churches that he was used to. Sure, Baptists might have a cross or a picture of Jesus but that was about it. Catholic churches were different. There were statues, tapestries, stained glass, candles. It was very reverent, which only added to the feeling that they were trespassing, even though they weren't.

They whispered to each other for fear of their voices echoing and bringing attention to themselves. Father Bishop was nice, but they didn't want to disturb him, and they didn't want to awkwardly admit they were just using the church to cool off.

"Hello, boys," Father Bishop said, which spooked and surprised them. Well, so much for not getting noticed. Apparently, the father was upstairs cleaning the balcony and watched the boys come in.

"Hello sir..."

"Hello Father..."

"Hello Mister..."

They all jumped and replied in such a haste that their reply came out all jumbled together.

"It's okay, boys. I know why you are here. You

are here to contemplate the universe and your role in it," he said, starting off seriously, then broke into a smile as he looked down at them and continued, "Or you are here to cool off? That's fine too; it's hot outside."

"Thanks!" they said in unison, then looked at each other in consternation. Chris then took the lead and said, "Thanks. We really appreciate it."

"Have a seat. I'm just going to continue to clean up here if that's all right with you boys," Father Bishop said.

They just nodded, as it was more a rhetorical question than anything. But now that they knew he was up there, they felt even more like they were trespassing. The cool air did feel refreshing and it was also nice to take a load off and sit down on the wooden pew. That was the one similarity Chris recognized between this church and the ones he was familiar with–the hard, wooden pews. It was surprising how comfortable they could be. The pews here were a dark, cherry wood, whereas the ones at the Baptist church were a light, golden oak, however they both felt the same.

They didn't stay very long. They had the feeling that they should be heading on, especially now that they knew that Father Bishop was upstairs. They didn't want to be a bother. Before they left, Chris yelled out to the father, "We're leaving. Thanks for letting us stick around."

Father Bishop stuck his head over the railing to watch them leave. "Okay, boys! Thanks for letting me know. Be careful and come back anytime!"

"Well, the padré seems like a nice guy," Brian said when they were beyond the church grounds.

"Yeah, I've never heard anything bad about him," Sam said.

"It's getting close to midday. We should probably be getting back to the house," Chris said.

They started the trek back to Aunt Christie's. It certainly hadn't gotten any cooler, but thankfully, the summer breeze made it bearable. They traveled the two-lane road back, occasionally switching sides as the cars came through, to make sure they had plenty of room. It didn't happen very often, but with the curves and hills, when they heard the sound of a motor coming up behind them, they changed sides as if they were on autopilot, without even mentioning it to one another.

It didn't take them more than 15 to 20 minutes to get to where they stashed their fishing gear and other stuff in the bushes. While retrieving it all, Chris noticed there was a folded piece of paper attached to his tackle box. It wasn't there before and he thought it very odd. How did it get there? He unfolded the note, and it was addressed to all of them. The penmanship was very neat. He read the contents before letting Sam and Brian read it.

"Boys: I noticed this morning, while you all were fishing at the pond, that you didn't catch anything. If you come tomorrow, I will teach you a little trick to catch more fish."

It wasn't signed, but it didn't take a brainiac to figure out who left the note. The boys were taken aback.

"How'd he find our stuff?" Brian said.

"Yeah, there's no way he saw us stash it," Sam said.

"I don't know," Chris replied.

Chris thought it very strange. Brian and Sam were right. There was no way anyone would have known about their hiding spot. At least the gear was still there, so he wasn't a thief.

"So, should we come back tomorrow?" Sam asked.

"I don't know," Chris said.

"Maybe we should. Maybe he really does have a trick. It would be nice to catch more fish," Brian said.

"Well, even if we don't, I am sure we will run into him again," Chris said, then turned toward Sam and asked, "How long did you say he's been around?"

"Not more than a few months, if that," he replied.

"Weird," Chris said.

"Weird," Brian and Sam echoed.

Chapter Five

The next morning, they went downstairs and got their things ready to go. The night before, they decided to go to the pond again. It wasn't so much because they wanted to learn a new fishing trick, though. The boys were intrigued and looked forward to discovering more about this newcomer that came in the form of the hermit. The boys let their aunt know where they were heading before they left the house. They hadn't told her or Uncle Bob about the encounter with the hermit at the pond or about the note that he left for them. They kept it to themselves so they wouldn't be told not to go meet up with him. The boys were curious and didn't want anything getting in the way. The morning was crisp, and the breeze was cool across Chris' face as they shut the door and headed across the yard toward the road. He knew, though, that it wouldn't last long because the heat of the day would rise just like it did the day before. This had always been his favorite time of day (or maybe a close second). He also enjoyed dusk, right as the sun was setting but before it got dark. The energy of the day transitioning into night, as well as the beauty of the last sun's rays reflecting on clouds as it disappeared around the curvature of the earth, always left an impression on him.

"You guys ready for this?" Chris asked.

"Why wouldn't I be?" Brian asked.

"Yeah, he is just a hermit," Sam said. "I just hope that he doesn't turn out to be a creep."

Chris had also thought of that and made sure to bring along his pocket knife. He usually carried it when going fishing because sometimes, lines needed to be cut. Today, he double-checked just to make sure. It wasn't a very large pocket knife, but it would hurt to get stabbed with and anything was better than nothing.

"Well, we will be sure to keep our distance," Chris said.

They continued and reached the pond in no time. There, at the far end was the hermit, already fishing. The hermit raised his hand in greeting then motioned for them to join him. The boys looked at each other one last time, in order to gather courage, then headed over. They stopped short about twenty feet away from the man. Now that they were closer, they could tell he was older, but they weren't sure. He had a weathered, suntanned face and dark eyes; although he had wrinkles, his face almost had an ageless look. With gray hair, which was almost white, and a close-cropped beard of the same shade, he looked like someone's grandpa one moment, then a younger version of the same man the next.

"Hello, boys," he said.

"How did you know where our stuff was yesterday?" Chris asked. Better to get that out of the way first, he thought to himself.

The hermit smiled. His teeth were straight and clean, not what one would expect when they thought of a hermit. He replied, "It was easy. Anyone could see the tracks going through the knee-high grass to those bushes, and I wanted to see what was back there. I saw your stuff and left the note."

The answer made sense to Chris but in looking back, he didn't remember leaving a trail. Then again, he wasn't a hunter and knew next to nothing about tracking.

"So, are ya here to learn about my fishing trick?" the hermit asked.

"I guess," Chris said.

"Yeah! Show us," Sam said excitedly. He was the only real fisherman of the group.

Brian just sort of shrugged in agreement and watched from a distance. He didn't really want to come this morning but came anyway because Chris and Sam wanted to. Being the youngest in a group, well, you just kind of do what the older kids do.

"Well, come a little closer so you can see," the hermit said as he smiled again, even bigger than before.

The boys got a little closer in order to watch. The hermit turned his fishing pole around, then took out something brown and hooked it on to the end of his hook.

"All right, boys...now watch me. Before I cast, I hold my rod in the air and make a circle, then throw it out." The hermit demonstrated, then followed through with casting.

It looked easy enough but not really all that different from what the boys did when they fished. Sure enough, though, within a minute, the hermit's arm jerked and he started reeling in a catch. He demonstrated a couple more times, just to make sure they really understood the technique.

"Okay, boys...now here's the secret. It's this brown root that I use as bait. The fish love it. By rotating it a full circle before throwing it out into the water, it lets the bait get a little more air," the hermit said and then continued, "I'm not sure why that helps but it does. It's very important; otherwise, it's only as good as any other bait, if that."

"That's wild," Sam said. "I've never seen a root like that. In fact, I don't think I've ever seen a root used as bait before. Where did you get it?"

"Ah, it only seems to grow up around my cabin," the hermit said.

"What's it called?" Chris asked.

"I don't know. I only know that it grows near where I live. I just decided to give it a try and lo and behold, it works," the hermit replied.

"Wow, what a find," Sam said.

The hermit reached down into his sack to get more of the brown root, then handed it out to the boys to try. The boys, in turn, did what he told them to do. They put the brown root on the hook and made an overhead circle before finally casting it out over the pond. Sure enough, within a few moments, they were each hauling their own fish out of the water.

"How strange," Chris thought to himself, "What a neat thing to learn." The root was nothing out of the ordinary in itself. It had a soft feel to it and was a bit chalky. As the dust from it rubbed off on his hand, he wiped it onto his jeans.

"And that's it," the hermit said. "That's the trick."

"That's really neat," Sam said. "So, this stuff only grows near where you live?"

"Yep. You all are welcome to come gather the stuff anytime you want. I don't mind company," the hermit said.

"Where do you live?" Sam asked.

"Across the street from the cemetery, at the top of the ridge...can't miss it," the hermit replied.

"What's your name?" Chris asked.

The hermit thought for a moment, looking off in the distance over the pond before replying, then said, "Oh, I haven't thought about my name in long time. Just call me Ol' Ned."

They started to introduce themselves but Ol' Ned interrupted them. "Oh, boys...I know your names already. I heard them all yesterday when you were talking to one another. You'd be surprised to know that I know a lot of different things."

He then smiled at them. Chris was a little taken aback as he didn't remember them talking so loudly yesterday. How could the hermit possibly have heard them?

The hermit replied, as if had read Chris' mind, "I have really good hearing as well."

Immediately, Chris felt like he didn't want to talk so loud anymore while around the hermit. He couldn't put his finger on it, but he felt something was amiss here, like looking at a picture where the proportions are slightly off; it's visibly imperceptible but the brain notices and doesn't tell. It was just a weird feeling that something wasn't quite right.

"That's awesome, Ned. Thanks for teaching us!" Sam said.

"My pleasure, Sam. I'm sure you all will return the favor at some point," Ned replied.

Ned let them take as much of the root as they wanted, then they all went back to fishing. They had no trouble catching fish; it seemed as soon as the bait hit the water, they were reeling in the catch. To Chris, it almost felt like cheating. If they were fishing to keep, they would have gone home long ago with buckets full of fish. But since they were throwing them back, it became a circle of activity–throw out the bait, catch, reel in, then throw back. After about thirty minutes, Chris was getting kind of bored and his hands were becoming tired from the constant motion of reeling in the fishing line.

Ol' Ned left not long after he showed them his trick. He filled up his container with all the fish he had caught. Chris thought to himself as he watched him leave, at this rate, the pond will soon be without any fish. In fact, if Ned had been fishing there more than a couple of days, he was surprised there were even any fish left to catch now.

As the next hour wore on, the fish seemed to quit biting, even with the special bait they were using. They were just about out of the bait, anyway, and it seemed like a good stopping point.

"Ready to go home?" Chris asked.

"Yeah," Brian said. "I'm ready to go do anything else."

"Me too," Sam added. "That was neat what that hermit showed us...but kind of takes all the fun out of it. It's kind of boring when you know you can't lose."

"I was thinking the same thing," Chris said. "Let's head through the farm to go home. We can stop by Gopher's gully on the way."

"Oh yeah," Brian said. "I'd like to see how that looks now."

Gopher's gully wasn't really a gully and wasn't much to look at. In fact, it was just a small indention in the land at the base of a hill; there were some trees that lined the small rift. The boys had built a small fort there after gathering fallen trees and logs that past storms had knocked down. They stacked the heavier logs on the bottom, then crisscrossed smaller logs and limbs in a way so that they intertwined, to construct a "fence." There was a large tree in the middle of the makeshift enclosure and although it didn't have an actual roof, they took other branches and made a lean-to type roof on one side of the fort, spanning from the fence to the tree. It wasn't much, but it provided extra shade under the canopy of the tree. It looked rickety, but it held. Of course, along the fence, there were gaping holes where the logs didn't lay flush with one another. The boys covered these holes with fresh, small limbs full of green leaves that they could easily reach and cut down. When they built it last summer, it was one of their favorite places to hang out. The lay of the land brought a good breeze and under the shade of the trees, it made it a very pleasant location. The fort itself was almost hard to find, especially in the first few weeks after being built, with the green leaves from the recently cut branches; they acted as perfect camouflage to cover the logs. It looked like another clump of bushes until you were inside the perimeter. No one knows who came up with the name "Gopher's gully." It was a nickname for sure, but they couldn't point to where the name came from. Every gang needed a hideout, and every Army unit needed a base, even pretend gangs and army units. During the last summer, they were full of imagination, doing army patrols and pretending to be attacked. It was just a name that came up and it stuck.

The boys left the pond and headed through the fields to reach their fort. As they walked, they continued in conversation about everything they hadn't talked about yet–all those things that young kids who haven't seen one another in a long time get together and talk about. It took a bit longer, walking over the uneven ground, but it was an adventure. Everything out here could be an adventure...or it could be supremely boring, thought Chris. He experienced both many times over the years in these fields. Even during the times of pretend adventures, the reality of wanting actual adventure would often play in the back of his mind.

They slowly made their way, hopping over fences that separated pastures and fields, being careful not to snag their most important body part on barbed wire as they crossed. This brought Chris back to a memory from third grade, which he laughed at now, but it was no laughing matter at that time. His whole class had been lined up to go to the cafeteria and he saw a waist-high, wooden pole and decided to leapfrog over it for some unknown reason. When he did, part of his pants got caught, ripping the entire seat seam, all the way down both legs, to the ankles. Thankfully, the wooden pole didn't catch anything else but going from wearing pants to wearing a dress with his underwear hanging out, was quite embarrassing for an eight-year-old boy. The teacher was gracious enough to help; she took him back into the classroom, away from everyone else and armed with several safety pins, patched his pants back together the best she could. He had never been so embarrassed in his life. Ever since, Chris practiced the utmost care when hopping or climbing over anything that neared the seat of his pants.

They crossed over the final hill and caught sight of the tree line below. It was a gentle slope so from their angle, they could see the remnants of Gopher's gully. They continued the rest of the way and as they got closer, they could see it was a former shell of what it once was. Even though it had only been a year since they built it, the months of disuse and being exposed to the elements had added up. The "roof" was gone, and one side of the fence had completely collapsed.

"Sam, did you ever come out here after we left last summer?" Brian asked.

"No. You guys weren't here, and I wasn't going to go traipsing over the farm by myself. That's no fun," Sam said.

Chris thought to himself that he probably wouldn't have either. It was weird seeing the fort as it was now, replacing the memories he made here the year before. Sometimes, things don't need to be revisited and just left as is. Otherwise, the new images and memories replace the old ones with stark change and most of the time, they are rarely good. All that work they did last year had gone to waste, quickly reclaimed by the land. Grass was waist-high in and around what was left of the fence structure.

After seeing the changes in the area, they weren't as interested in sticking around or creating new memories here.

"I'm ready to get back to the house," Chris said.

"Yeah, me too," Brian said glumly, looking over Gopher's gully.

The boys gave the area one more look of finality and headed on. Their feelings of disappointment eventually turned back into a good mood as the conversation evolved into discussions about what else they wanted to get into this summer.

"Hey, we should walk down and visit Erin," Brian said.

"You guys can, but I think I may stick around the house and do something else," Chris said.

"Oh, come on..." Brian pleaded.

"No, I'm not interested," Chris said.

Chris was thinking about the previous summers when his crush on Erin's older sister, Jessica had become more pronounced. He would go on long walks that happened to include passing right in front of their house, hoping that they would be outside or maybe see him and come out to say "Hello." That actually happened once or twice but nothing ever really came of it except for a wave or hello, or maybe a small, superficial conversation. For long, summer days in the country, any distraction like that was a good one. Of course, that was during the days when Brian and Sam didn't notice girls, so he walked alone. Then again, he didn't really invite them; he would wait until they were doing something and leave without telling them. Who knows? Jessica may have been interested, but Chris was too shy and afraid to follow through and find out one way or the other, so all the meetings were nothing more than just pleasantries. This summer, with Jessica having a boyfriend, he didn't want to waste his time or get frustrated.

"What if..." Brian started.

"No," Chris interrupted, not even bothering to hear what he was going to say.

Brian sighed with resignation, "Fine..."

When they got back to the house, it was around noon. They ate a lunch that consisted of sandwiches and chips, then washed it down with soda. The rest of the day was spent goofing off. Uncle Bob was at work and Aunt Christie was in town visiting friends, so it was just the three of them.

"Do you want to head up to the hermit's house and pick some of those roots?" Sam asked. "I mean…we ran out today while fishing and it would be nice to have some when we go again."

"I don't know," Chris said.

"Oh, come on. The hermit…uh…Ol' Ned, even invited us to," Sam said.

"Even if we don't get roots, we can still go see where he lives," Brian said. "It'll be an adventure, and at the very least, it'll give us something to do."

Chris thought it over and it would be something to go do. He did wonder what the hermit's place looked like. He'd been all over that hill in the past and was curious as to where it was.

"Ok, but we'll wait 'til Aunt Christie gets home before we go," he said.

Chapter Six

It wasn't long after the boys decided to go visit the hermit that Aunt Christie pulled into the driveway. They went on their way after telling her they were going to go exploring. The hill where the hermit apparently lived was slightly over a half mile away, not far from the pond where they fished. It was one of the many rolling foothills that dotted the area and led to the Ozarks in Missouri. The hill, or ridge, was a couple of miles long and was the same one that overlooked Stonemill. It rose a couple hundred feet and had steep inclines in some areas; those were hard to see since the whole area was heavily wooded. Chris and his little band of adventurers had been all over that ridge at different times over the years during his continued summer visits, so it wasn't an unknown area to them by any stretch of the imagination.

They arrived at the pond where they had been that morning. It was strange how an area could look totally different depending on the time of day and weather. A place that is and was familiar could suddenly look foreign. Chris turned his gaze from over the pond up to the wooded hill. There were no noticeable trails to follow and it was dense where the woods met the road. It looked almost like a wall of trees and underbrush, like some forgotten fortress that implied the message, "Keep out."

67

They started forward and once the boys broke through the protective barrier, it immediately opened and wasn't as dense under the tree canopy. The groundcover wasn't thick, because shadow from the treetops and the carpet of dead leaves didn't allow for much growth. It was strangely quiet–not even the birds were singing their summer songs, nor did they hear the movement of small critters running through the woods. It was just after the hottest part of the day and things were usually sluggish around this time, but Chris could never remember it being that quiet. When the boys noticed the silence, they spoke in hushed whispers, as though that was required for their right to be there.

"Where do you think it is?" Sam whispered.

"He said it was at the top of hill," Brian answered quietly.

Sam rolled his eyes and whispered back, "I know what he said but it's a pretty dang large hill."

"I'm pretty sure it's straight up," Chris said, "and why are we whispering?"

Sam shrugged and said, "I don't know. It just felt like the right thing to do."

Brian looked like he was about to answer but after hearing Sam's reply and seeing his shrug, he looked at Chris and shrugged, too, not saying a word.

"Well, let's stop whispering. We don't want anyone to think we are trying to sneak up on them," Chris said.

They nodded but didn't say anything more as they

ventured deeper into the forest and higher in elevation as the ground sloped upwards. They eventually came upon a small footpath that looked like it had recently been made. It was a little smaller than a deer trail, likely because it hadn't had the chance to develop from heavier or constant travel. They were halfway to the top and continued forward on the footpath, which made it much easier since they didn't have to be quite as conscious in putting their feet down with each step. Off the trail, the boys had to be more watchful of larger roots or fallen tree limbs that could cause them to trip.

Soon, they noticed the aroma of smoke and cooking food wafting through the air. Even though they had just eaten lunch before they started on this journey, whatever they were smelling got their mouths watering. They thought maybe they could eat just a little something more…that is, if there was something up ahead for them to eat.

The smell got stronger as they headed forward, not in an overpowering way, but they could definitely tell someone was cooking nearby. They soon came into the area where the wonderful aroma originated. It was a clearing small enough so the that the overhead tree canopy still covered a significant portion of it. It was flat and large enough to have a small, well-made cabin and in front of the cabin, a small fire pit with what looked like a makeshift grill grate placed over the flames. It had larger logs set up around the fire where someone could sit and enjoy it. Chris had never seen this place before and was honestly surprised where it was located. He could have sworn he had been through this area in previous years, but he certainly didn't recognize it now. It had a quaint, welcoming atmosphere to it. The hermit, or rather Ol' Ned, was bent over the fire, preoccupied with cooking whatever was giving off that awesome smell. When he noticed the boys, he straightened up and spoke.

"Come, come on over. I knew you boys would be coming. Please sit down." He waved his arms in a welcoming gesture, indicating toward the logs for them to sit.

"Yes, I knew you would come, and I have made extra food. You must be hungry," Ol' Ned continued.

It smelled inviting and it reminded them that yes, they were a bit hungry, but Chris hadn't expected all of this. "What is it?" he asked.

"Oh, the way I cook things, it can be whatever you want it to be," the hermit replied.

It looked like fish to Chris and with the way he felt about fish, or any seafood for that matter...Well, he wasn't going to go out of his way to eat it, even if he was hungry. He only enjoyed catching them; he had no desire to eat them.

"I see that look in your eye, Chris. It's okay. I promise it will be one of the best meals you've ever had."

As soon as they sat down, the hermit pulled out plates with forks and handed them to the boys. The plates were made from highly polished wood, as well as the forks. Chris, not knowing a thing about woodworking, marveled at the quality of the items.

He'd seen worse at the local flea market back home in Florida fetch decent prices. This was definitely not what he expected to find here.

The hermit scraped what was on the grill into a wooden bowl, which was also of high quality. He then picked up a pot that was closer to the fire and poured contents from that into the bowl. He mixed it up and then served it to the boys, as well as putting a serving on his own plate.

Chris looked down and saw bits of white meat mixed in with what looked to be rice and some sort of brown gravy mixture. He wasn't hungry when he started the trip to get here but now, he was famished and couldn't wait to dig in. It was a hunger that went beyond normal. It was almost a feeling of starvation, with hunger pangs that nearly throbbed all the way to his spine.

He looked around the group and they were all digging in. Funny, but when they first arrived, it didn't look like there'd be enough food to go around, but there was more than enough to fill everyone's plate. He hesitantly took his first bite, expecting some foul, fishy taste, but what he tasted was something completely unexpected. He tasted his favorite meal, which was steak with just the right amount of seasoning. It tasted just like what his mom made for him on his birthday. "How strange," Chris thought. What he was eating looked nothing like what it tasted; each bite was just as savory as the first. The plate was clean before long. Chris looked down at it in surprise (and also a little remorse) that the experience of eating such a fine meal was over so soon.

Also, just as surprising, he realized he wasn't stuffed either. They had eaten before they set out to find the hermit's cabin and should have already been full before even starting this meal. Chris looked around and saw that the plates in Brian's and Sam's laps were clean, as well.

"That was fantastic," Brian said.

"Yes. That was great," Sam said.

Chris didn't say anything. He was taking in the whole scene and looking all around him. The cabin wasn't just well-made; it was built with the same exquisite quality and detail as the plates. From the outside, it looked to be a single-room space. The logs were expertly laid and fit together like a puzzle. It reminded Chris of the Lincoln Logs that he used to play with as a kid. It even had a front porch with an awning and windows with real glass. It was very picturesque and in the back of Chris' mind, he wondered how the hermit was able to build such a structure by hand, without construction equipment. There were no roads or large trails that would even accommodate such equipment that Chis could see. The voice of Ol' Ned brought him back to the conversation.

"I knew you would like it," the hermit said.

"Yeah. It was pretty good," Chris said.

Continuing to look around, Chris asked curiously, "How did you build all this? I don't see where you got the logs for your cabin. There are no tree stumps that I can see nearby."

"Oh...You have a good eye," the hermit said, then he looked around at his handiwork before continuing. "I know a thing or two about woodworking and building. I've been around a long time and I've picked up a few things over the years."

Chris noticed Brian and Sam were now looking around at the cabin and the plates in their hands. They looked at the plates like they were examining a new bug they had discovered. Chris was aware of how sometimes, things surprise people when it is brought to their attention and in Brian and Sam's case, it was no different. The mental calculations that were rolling around Chris' mind didn't equate to what he saw in front of him as being built by one man alone.

"You did it all yourself?" Chris asked, indicating the cabin.

"Yes, I did. Like I said, I have a lot of knowledge and tricks up my sleeve," the hermit responded.

Chris was genuinely impressed. "That's amazing," Chris said, "May I look inside?"

"Sure. Go right ahead." The hermit then said to all the boys, "Leave your plates right where you are. I'll pick them up later to clean."

"Are you sure?" Brian asked, "I mean, we can clean them."

"No...no...that's fine. You all are guests here," the hermit replied.

"Well..." Brian became uncomfortable, feeling that he should have at least cleaned the plate but said, "Thanks."

Chris put his plate to the side, stood up, and then walked toward the cabin, hopping up onto the front porch. He didn't go inside because he didn't want to intrude too much, so he stayed on the porch and looked in. The inside looked just as nice and out of place as the outside. He saw bookshelves lined with leather-bound books that looked very old but well-kept. Definitely not the type of stuff you'd expect to find at some hermit's cabin in the woods.

"What kind of books are those?" Chris asked.

"Oh, I've picked up many different books over the years and those are very old. I may be considered a hermit...Oh, I know that's what you boys think I am, but I'm also a collector of many things."

Curiosity piqued, "What are they about?"

"I doubt you'd be interested. Mostly stuff related to nature–plants and other things–but they are all written in different languages, primarily Latin," Ol' Ned replied.

"Yep. Definitely not something you'd expect to find in the woods around here," Chris thought. He then remembered the reason why they had come here in the first place.

"I almost forgot. Where are those plants with the roots you fish with? We'd like to pick some, if that's all right," Chris said.

"Oh, sure. You can pick as much as you want, but I forgot to tell you they are only good right after you pick them. After a few hours, they don't seem to work anymore. Come on–let me show you where they are," the hermit said.

He took them to the side of the cabin and sure enough, there was a small field of wild, multicolored flowers with the deepest shades of red, yellow and even blue. Chris had never before seen a plant with such vibrant flowers. The hermit went over and grabbed one by the stem and gave a sharp tug. The flower came out of the ground and a little bulb with roots was still attached to the bottom and caked with dirt. The hermit brushed off the dirt, showing the same root the boys saw earlier. He then plucked the root free from the rest of the plant. Chris thought he might be seeing things but it almost looked as if the flower immediately lost its vibrancy once the root was detached. He didn't get a good look because the hermit tossed the flower into the woods, like trash.

"And here you go," the hermit said, handing the root to Chris and looking over at all of the boys. "That's how you do it. A quick pull, wipe off the dirt, and it's ready to go. But remember…it's only good for a couple hours. Best to pick it right before you plan to fish."

Chris put the root into his pocket and then noticed the sun was a lot farther down in the sky than he thought it should be. It wasn't quite dusk, but give it another hour and it would be. Just how long had they been here? By Chris' estimation, it was only an hour or maybe two, but looking at the sky through the trees, the sun was just above the horizon, whereas it had been overhead when they arrived. He looked at his watch and it was just past six-thirty. "What? How?" Chris thought to himself, confused. They left the house at around two and couldn't have been here more than a couple hours, at the most, but clocks don't lie. They had been here about four hours.

"We gotta go," Chris said.

"So soon?" the hermit asked.

"Yeah. Look at the time. We've been here longer than I thought." Chris said.

The hermit looked around and said, "That can happen sometimes."

The surprise showed in Brian and Sam's faces as they looked at their watches, then at each other with the same expressions Brian imagined he had when he realized the time.

"Wow! Yeah–we gotta go. Mom's gonna be worried," Sam said.

Before they left, they thanked Ol' Ned for the food. The hermit said they could come visit anytime they felt like it. As he watched them leave, he saw a squirrel scurry toward the woods. He turned his attention and gestured for the squirrel to come to him. The squirrel came closer and closer. It was the same squirrel that he encountered on the road a couple of weeks ago. He knew because he was able to distinguish all the nearby creatures by sight. He reached down and grabbed the squirrel, startling it. His smile took on a more sinister look as he cupped its little body in his hands. An odd, bright blue and dull red glow emanated from his hands. When he took his hand away, the lifeless body of the squirrel remained; its eyes were liquid pools of night that stared aimlessly toward the hermit. His gaze returned to the retreating forms of the boys as they left. His smile grew in size, almost like that of a caricature one would have drawn by an artist while on vacation. This smile, however, brought no joy. It looked heinous, grotesque and out of place. The boys were almost out of his sight now. He took the squirrel's body and bit it in half. The bones crunched in his mouth as he chewed. He swallowed and the rest of the squirrel disappeared into the horrible visage. A moment later, the boys were out of view and the hermit's face returned to normal. He smiled once more toward the boys' direction before he turned to go into his cabin.

The boys were halfway home as they talked about what a great meal it was. "Yeah, I think that was the best steak I've ever tasted," Chris said.

"Steak?" Brian questioned, then continued, "That tasted like the best pizza I've ever had."

"What are you guys talking about? That was Italian beef," Sam said, mentioning his favorite food.

"Wait–you tasted pizza and you tasted Italian beef?" Chris asked.

"Yes," came the reply in unison.

Something weird was definitely going on, Chris thought, and he didn't think he liked it. It just felt "off" and deep down in his soul, a warning bell started to ring a soft chime. Chris stopped walking as he reached into his pocket for the root and pulled it out. As he looked down, it crumbled to dust in his hand, leaving nothing in its place.

"I don't think we should hang out with Ol' Ned," he said as they continued the rest of the way home.

Chapter Seven

They arrived back to the house just as the sun was slipping behind the hills. The day went from vibrant colors to the muted gray that separates day and night. The boys walked through the front door and Aunt Christie was at the kitchen table, waiting for them. She had a serious, but grateful expression on her face. Thankfully, Uncle Bob wasn't home yet, because he had to stay at work to deal with a small emergency, the boys later found out. Otherwise, they would have had to have dealt with him. Aunt Christie could be stern at times, but Uncle Bob could be so stern it was downright scary.

"Where have you boys been?" she asked. "You had me worried."

The boys looked at each other and then back to her. They then explained what had occurred that afternoon to keep them from coming home sooner. It was true that they had freedom to run to the ends of the earth as long as they checked in every so often. It wasn't okay to be gone for hours at a time unless of course, there was activity and location that could be accounted for.

"I'm sorry. We lost track of time but honestly, Aunt Christie, it wasn't something we were actively trying to do. It was like time skipped," Chris started to explain.

"Yeah, Mom," Sam said, "We ran across the hermit in the woods across from the pond and he invited us to eat. It smelled so good."

Brian then started, adding to the explanation, "And after we ate, time sort of got away from us."

Aunt Christie listened to them tell their story and after the boys finished, she took it in and thought about it, as if weighing it on a scale of justice to see if it balanced. It must have, because she replied, "Well, I'm glad you boys are okay, but next time, be sure to check in regularly."

"We know," Chris said.

"And I don't think I want you boys hanging out with the hermit," she continued.

"That's okay with us," Chris said, looking at the other two boys and speaking for them all. "I mean, he was nice, but it was kind of strange."

"What do you mean?" Aunt Christie asked.

"I don't know. The meal was great, and the hermit was nice but..." Chris started before being interrupted by Sam who said, "Everything seemed fine to me."

Chris looked at Sam, then back to Aunt Christie, "Well, it was fine, but I don't think we will be going out of our way to go visit."

"That food sure was good, though," Brian said.

Chris agreed with him, but it was a strange experience, for sure.

"Well, I don't want you boys going back there," she said with finality, in such a way that they knew the subject was no longer open for discussion. This was just fine with Chris.

"By the way, boys...did you hear that there is going to be a carnival in town?" Aunt Christie reported.

"Really?" Sam asked.

"That's never happened before," Chris said. Sure, there had been carnivals and festivals in other towns nearby, but Stonemill had never had an actual carnival come to town. The closest thing the town ever saw was a small festival every August, which was little more than a farmers market with local community members setting up booths, with games like "Pop the Balloon" with Uncle Wilmer's or cousin Jay's personal dart set.

"When?" Brian asked.

"I think I heard it'll be this weekend, and it will be here for a few days or so," Aunt Christie said.

"Oh neat! I can't wait," Sam said, excitedly.

Chris thought the prospect of a carnival would be a fun event to look forward to. In his experience, usually during the summers here in southern Illinois, there were no events beyond the normal, scheduled ones like going to church weekly or the occasional spontaneous trips to Bell Smith Springs or Lake Thunderhawk, local swimming holes. He still couldn't shake that nagging feeling that something was wrong, though. There were too many unexpected, unexplained recent events and although they hadn't been bad experiences, it still nagged at him. As the night wore on, he became accustomed to the feeling and pretty soon, he no longer noticed it.

The week was uneventful. They stayed away from the pond and from fishing. They, or rather Chris, didn't want to unexpectedly run into the hermit again. Aunt Christie did tell them to avoid him, so he made sure they did. They went to church Wednesday night and the Darling sisters were there. Erin came over and talked with Brian and Sam, while Jessica stayed in her seat. She nodded to them but didn't seem all that interested. Church wasn't going to start for another ten minutes and the sanctuary was cold, so he got up to go say "Hi" to her and to warm up a little.

"Hey, Jessica," Chris said. "How are things going?"

"I've had better weeks," she said.

"Oh? Everything okay?" Chris asked.

"Yeah. My boyfriend and I broke up this week. I found out he was seeing another girl. What a jerk," she said.

"I'm so sorry," Chris said.

"It's okay. I was thinking of breaking up with him anyway. He was kind of a jerk, so it was a relief when I found out. I mean…I'm not happy about it but at least we didn't get too serious before I found out," she said then asked, "So what about you? How is your summer going so far?"

"Oh, about as usual," he said. "Although, we did

run into a hermit that lives in the woods overlooking Stonemill. That was kinda weird, but nothing too crazy."

"Oh really?" she said. "That's interesting, because if it's the same guy, my dad was having issues with one of our horses a couple of days ago. I wasn't there but he was telling us later during dinner about what had happened. Anyway, Dad was out in the pasture with Rocket–that's the horse's name–near the road, and he wasn't doing well. Rocket had been lethargic the past couple of days and when my dad went out to check on him, he found him on the ground laying there and he wouldn't get back up. He was beginning to think that he may have to put Rocket down, but then this guy comes out of nowhere and asked my dad if he could take a look at the horse. My dad thought it was weird, but not having any better options, said 'sure'."

"Oh my!" Chris said, totally engrossed. "What happened next?"

"Well, he told us that the man came into the pasture and asked my dad to go grab a bucket of water, which again, my dad thought was weird, but whatever...he went back to the barn to get it. When he came back, Rocket was standing there, just as fit as a fiddle. Nothing appeared wrong with him at all. My dad said that it shocked him. He'd been near horses all his life and had never seen such a thing. The old man told my dad when he got back that there wasn't anything really wrong. He said it was just a long splinter that needed to be removed. We all went out to check on Rocket from time to time and we never saw a splinter. Anyway, Dad asked him if he needed anything and the man said, no, not this time around. Then he left the pasture and continued walking down the road. Weird, huh?" Jessica said, finishing her story.

"Totally," Chris replied, "Did you happen to see him?"

"No, I didn't. In fact, I wouldn't have thought of it at all until you said something and if my dad wasn't so animated when he talked about it. You know my dad. He's a very reserved kind of guy so anytime he talks excitedly about something, it's something," she said, and laughed.

This was true. Jessica's dad was very reserved. Chris didn't think he exchanged more than a few words with him in all the years that he visited. Even when they had talked in the past, Jessica's dad spoke with a very low voice, sometimes to the point of being inaudible. Chris, wanting to be polite, often avoided conversation with him so he didn't have to keep asking him to repeat himself since he couldn't hear or understand what he said.

Church was about to start and her sister Erin, as well as her mom, had finished with visiting other church members and returned to the pew where Jessica was sitting. Jessica's dad didn't come on Wednesday nights and neither did Uncle Bob, for that matter.

"Hello, Mrs. Darling," Chris said as he was getting up to head back to where Aunt Christie, Sam, and his brother were sitting.

"Hello, Chris. I haven't seen you walking the road in front of our house this summer yet," she said, smiling at him.

You could definitely tell they were family. Mrs. Darling had wavy, dark brown hair and fair skin, as well. All the ladies of the Darling family looked like a slightly different version of one another.

"Oh, yeah...uh...probably later this summer when there's nothing else to do," Chris said absentmindedly, and immediately felt awkward about saying such a thing. He felt like he had to say something and that was the first thing that came to mind. He could feel his face flush but quickly got out of the situation before it lingered on. "Talk to you all after church!" he said, as he abruptly turned around, not waiting for a reply. He hoped they didn't notice his red face as he walked back to where he planned to sit for the service.

"Why is your face red?" Brian asked him when he sat down.

"Shut up," Chris replied.

Brian just rolled his eyes at him and went back to doodling on a donation envelope that he had taken from the pew in front of him. Service started shortly after Chris sat down, beginning with Mrs. Maple, a long-time church member, playing the piano. The preacher's wife stood near her, picking up the hymnal to lead the worship portion of church. Wednesday night service was just like Sunday morning and Sunday evening service, except not nearly as well-attended. Sunday Evening attendance was hit or miss for the small town, but it was still bigger than Wednesday night's. Chris looked around the sanctuary and there was plenty of room between the different families that were there this evening. Half of the attendees were seniors and had been members of the church for a very long time. Chris couldn't remember a time when they weren't here. There was another woman near the front with a child of about five, who brought his toy cars and used the pew as an imaginary dirt track.

Mr. Williams, who looked every bit the epitome of "country preacher," began the service as usual, with prayer. "Please stand and turn to page 335," his wife said when he finished with the prayer.

Everyone stood up and began to sing. They sang two songs and before the actual preaching portion of the service began, announcements were made, not that there were many. It was brother Tom Johnson's sixty-eighth birthday today but he wasn't there tonight, so they quickly moved on. Then came time for prayer requests. One of the older ladies up front stood and said one of her grandkids was sick, then sat down. It looked like that was about to be it for the prayer request portion but before it was over, Mr. Williams spoke up as he took out a handkerchief and wiped his face. "Well, it seems our bell in the steeple has quit ringing and I don't know when it will get fixed. I don't have the equipment to even go inspect it and you all know that the church doesn't have much in the way of resources, so please keep it in your prayers," he said, before folding the handkerchief and putting it back into his pocket.

The preaching portion of service began, and it was on par with all the other experiences that Chris had had when it came to listening to sermons at this church. It was short and earnest, with points being made that built on one another like small waves crashing on the shore. The waves gradually grew, with one or two large waves to finish the point of the message. Then it was over–calm seas again, then alter call. With this small crowd of dedicated members, the alter call didn't last very long at all.

As they were filing out into the parking lot, Brian and Sam were talking excitedly about the carnival that was coming to town this weekend. Chris listened in and apparently, they were talking with Erin about it before church and the Darling sisters planned to make an appearance. It was all but confirmed when Erin told Brian and Sam that she'd see them this weekend, as she got into her family's car, which was parked right beside Aunt Christie's beat-up farming truck, and shut the door.

Chris hopped into the bed of the truck and turned his head to look at the Darling car. His eyes briefly met Jessica's eyes as they backed out of the parking space. It wasn't quite dark yet; the sun was still high enough to be able to see clearly. Chris smiled a self-conscious smile and nodded, which was returned before the Darlings' car rolled forward and out of his sight.

"So, I guess we are meeting them at the carnival?" Chris asked his brother.

Brian looked back at him with a look that was equivalent to an eye-roll and said, "Well...yeah." As if that response actually answered the real questions that Chris had: how the conversation came about, how it got planned, etc. But nope, no answer to those questions, only a "yeah."

"Whatever," Chris responded, and settled down in the bed of the truck as Aunt Christie backed out of the parking space and then pulled forward to leave.

"What?" Brian asked. "I answered your question."

Chris just ignored both Brian and Sam for the rest of the ride home. It wasn't really that important and he didn't want to waste any more energy talking about it.

Brian and Sam sat and talked about upcoming plans. They excitedly discussed games they wanted to play, rides they wanted to ride, and carnival food they wanted to eat.

"I'm going to get a candy apple!" Sam said.

"Funnel cake for sure!" Brian said.

"Ugh..." thought Chris. With funnel cake, the first bite was heaven but that slowly sunk into the last bite being a form of culinary hell. He couldn't remember the last time he actually finished one. Usually about halfway through, he'd have to throw it in the trash. It also didn't help that after you finished eating it, you looked like a coke addict with all the powdered sugar that came on top.

"We'll ride all the rides...the Ferris wheel and, well, whatever else they have," Sam said.

"Yeah, we will definitely ride the Scrambler, if

they have it," Brian said, thinking of his favorite ride at the state fair last year. It was a ride that spun in a clockwise motion with several smaller cars that would spin independently. You'd always end up getting scrunched together (or maybe scrambled?) with other riders, due to centrifugal force.

There was no telling how big or small this traveling show would be this weekend. Who knew what they would or would not have. One thing was for sure though, as Chris listened to Brian and Sam make plans, knowing that Jessica Darling would be there made him look a little more forward to it.

Chapter Eight

The two days between Wednesday and Friday, when the carnival was supposed to arrive and start setting up, seemed like the longest two days in Chris' young life. Sometimes, the mere act of looking forward to an event stretches the time out in a way that can't really be explained, although everyone understands it.

Thursday lagged by and when Friday morning arrived, Chris thought walking down to the Stonemill country store would be a good idea, because 1) he just wanted to get out of the house and 2) to see if the carnival was in the village setting up. They told Aunt Christie where they were heading and left. They walked down the lane; the boys kicked rocks on the gravel road as they went, which sent rocks careening down to the road to hit other rocks, like a game of marbles knocking other marbles around.

During his many travels down this particular stretch on the way to town, Chris would often spend time looking for flatter rocks to skip across the pond. The boys would have competitions of which one could make the rock skip the most times across. One time last year, Chris skipped the rock fifteen times, which was a magnificent feat. Neither he nor the other two boys had even come close to that number since.

He then had a weird thought: he wondered how many skips Jessica could make. Strangely, those fleeting, random thoughts that included Jessica crept up more in his mind over the past couple of days, especially since she told him that she had broken up with her boyfriend. That was another strange thing about life, Chris noticed–how just a little bit of hope for opportunity can take over a person's focus, little by little. But as quickly as the thought of Jessica came, it was gone, as these kinds of thoughts seemed to do.

They had totally forgotten about the hermit, with the attention spans of young boys being what they are. The boys focused only on things that were in front of them and since they weren't planning on hanging out with the hermit anytime soon, they gave him no more thought. The hermit, on the other hand, hadn't forgotten about the boys or anyone else, for that matter. If the boys had been paying attention and looked up into the woods, they might have seen that Ol' Ned was watching them as they passed below him. His eyes appeared abnormally large, not keeping with the usual visage that others saw when they looked at him. Since he was alone, he let himself go a bit. No need to pay attention to looks when he was alone…besides, he was focusing on the boys. He was listening to their conversation, even long after they passed. He could still hear them chatter with one another, long after a typical human's sense of hearing would allow. After the boys disappeared down the road and around the curve, and the sound dwindled from the hermit's ears, he started to parallel the boys, keeping to the hill above them.

A few minutes later, Chris and the other two boys descended into the town, passing the Catholic church on the way. Chris always thought about how scenic the location of the church was, as he walked past. It was situated on a hill, overlooking the town and the valley. It wasn't high on the large hill, which continued across the street from the church and continued on up to the peak. But it was a good spot where the view of the ground sloping away to the west gave the impression of a larger vista than what it really was. Father Bishop was outside and waved at the boys. They returned the wave and continued on.

They walked through the heart of the village and made it to the store. This time though, both the front, wooden door with a window, and the screen door were closed. The "open" sign attached to the window beckoned and reminded people passing that the store was still open for business. Chris could only think of the stifling air that was inside, remembering the last time they were there. "Well, this is unexpected," thought Chris as they opened the door and felt a wave of cool air blanketing them almost immediately. A small bell jingled, welcoming them and notifying everyone in the store that visitors were arriving. They overheard faint voices coming from the back of the store.

"I'll be right with you!" Chris heard a yell from the back of the store, then the voice continued in lower volume, presumably to someone closer.

"Thank you so much for fixing that. The repair guy that normally comes said we'd have to replace the whole unit and, well…that wasn't going to happen.

It's been out for a while already." Chris recognized the voice as that of Mrs. Willing who waited on them last time they came in.

Chris could hear the low strum of an air conditioning unit. That certainly wasn't working the last time they were here. Mrs. Willing continued, "Yeah, I thought the unit was done. Not sure what you did, but you are a life saver."

The boys continued into the depths of the store where the rows of goodies awaited them. From around the shelves, Chris saw her come from the back, followed by someone else. "Ol' Ned?! What's he doing here?" Chris thought to himself.

"What did you do to fix it?" the lady asked Ol' Ned.

"Oh, nothing at all, surprisingly. It was just a screw loose in a couple of places. Really, it was nothing at all," Ol' Ned replied with a smooth smile. Ol' Ned looked over the store and saw Chris and the other two boys.

"Oh, hello boys. I haven't seen you in a few days," he said with the same smile.

Chris wasn't sure and he couldn't quite say why, but like a rock skipping across the water, a thought crossed his mind like a revelation when he saw Ol' Ned. The smile on his face didn't quite reach his eyes. It was as if his smile and his face were two separate entities that didn't belong together. It was very subtle, but the more Chris noticed it, the more it unnerved him. He unexpectedly shivered with goosebumps. "Oh great," Chris thought, "Someone is walking over my grave," thinking of the idiom that people often use when that happens.

Brian was farther inside the store and closest to Ol' Ned, so he answered, "Oh, hi…uh…we've been busy." This was a half answer and not really the truth because they certainly hadn't been busy, but the hermit wouldn't know any different, would he?

Ol' Ned's eyes turned toward Brian, "Oh, I see," he replied.

Mrs. Willing interrupted, totally oblivious to the attempt at conversation, "Well, if you hadn't come in this morning and fixed the air, we'd all be sitting here taking another shower in sweat. How much do I owe you?"

The hermit's smile disappeared, and his attention went back to the clerk. "Oh, it was nothing. I don't want anything…right now."

"Are you sure?" she asked.

"I'm sure. All in due time…all in due time," he said. His smile came back as his eyes glistened. She wasn't sure what that meant but she was so grateful that she didn't have to sit in the sweltering heat of the store that she had unwillingly become accustomed to. This guy could have danced the jig in front of her and she wouldn't have given it much thought.

Ol' Ned then turned, taking the whole store in, and announced, "Well, I must be on my way. I have things to do."

As he passed Chris, he winked as his smile got larger and said, "Be sure to come get some more root before you all go fishing."

Chris didn't say anything. His mind was reeling with just how peculiar this guy was. With the momentary lapse of conversation, the hermit continued, "Well, have a good day boys. I'll see you soon."

He walked out the front door, closed it and the outside screen door banged shut. Chris watched his shadow disappear to the side of the window. A sense of curiosity rose in the center of his young mind. He walked to the door to look out the window. He wanted to see where the hermit was heading. Nope...didn't see him. Weird.

"Brian, Sam, y'all stay here. I will be right back," Chris said, as he opened the front door to go outside.

"Okay," he heard them say behind him, as the door shut. He was out in front of the store. He turned his gaze far into the distance both ways and across the street. Except for a couple cars either coming or going, the streets were empty. He saw no figures walking. The brick building that the store was in wasn't very large. Chris thought maybe the hermit turned one of the corners and that's why he didn't see him. He just left the store; he couldn't have gotten far. Chris walked quickly to one side of the building. Nope, he wasn't there. He then walked to the other side. There was no sign of Ol' Ned anywhere.

"Well...this is weird," Chris thought to himself. He stood outside a bit longer before turning and heading back inside the store. His brother was at the counter, paying for his drink. He looked at Chris as he came through the front door. "You okay?" Brian asked.

"Yeah, why do you ask?" Chris asked.

"I don't know. You look like you're thinking really hard about something," Brian responded.

"Yeah...I don't know. The hermit–he just disappeared. I didn't see him anywhere outside," Chris said.

Brian glanced from Chris to the door and then to the front window of the store to look outside. He then turned back to Mrs. Willing behind the counter and completed his purchase. He grabbed his can of cola, said "thanks" and walked over to Chris.

"Yeah. I don't know if you've noticed, but there is something..." Brian said, stopping to search for the right word, "'off' about that guy. I think we should do what Aunt Christie said and stay away from him."

Sam went up to the counter and paid for his drink, then joined the rest of the group. "What are y'all whispering about over here?"

"The importance of listening to your mother," Brian said, which was totally lost on Sam. "And we weren't whispering."

"Uh...okay. Y'all ready, then?" Sam asked, not really following the conversation but ready to get moving on to whatever was next.

"One sec. Let me grab something," Chris said.

He darted over to the stand-alone drink cooler that stood against the wall, to grab his own drink. He then went to pay for it. Out of curiosity, he asked Mrs. Willing, "Do you know that guy? I mean…have you ever seen him before?"

"Who?" she asked.

He looked at her, confused. "That guy that just left. The one who fixed your air conditioner."

Now she returned his confused look with one of her own. "What are you talking about? Is there something wrong with the air conditioner?"

"It was broken, right?" Chris offered, totally surprised with the direction that this conversation turned.

"Air conditioner broken? Oh, my goodness. I hope not. That would be miserable. Could you imagine?" she said, smiling, but in a way that implied "Okay, kid–move along. This conversation is weirding me out."

"So…no one came in just before we came in? There wasn't someone else here?" he asked.

"It's been a slow morning. All I've seen is you three," she said, then looked down at the can of cola, "That will be fifty cents."

Dumbfounded, Chris looked down at his drink and remembered why he was there. He numbly handed over the dollar then waited for the change as his mind was racing, trying to understand what had just happened.

Concerned, Mrs. Willing asked him if he was all right.

"Yes ma'am. Thank you," Chris said on autopilot as he retrieved his change. He then hurried over to his brother and cousin, wanting to leave the store as quickly as he could. Whatever was going on, he wanted to be as far away as possible from it.

They left the store and as the front door shut, leaving the cool air inside, they heard Mrs. Willing tell them to have a good day. Well, it had been good, but now it had turned weird, Chris thought. He didn't say anything. He stayed on the sidewalk and just kept walking…with a purpose. The other boys began to protest a little, asking him to slow down, but it didn't register in the ears of the older boy. When they were clear of the store and about a block away, Chris slowed and turned to Brian and Sam.

"Did you guys hear that? She didn't remember the hermit," Chris said.

"No. What do you mean?" his brother asked.

Chris explained what happened at the counter and the two other boys looked at him with suspicion. "Are you pulling our leg?" Sam asked.

"No!" Chris said, "It sounds crazy, but I'm telling the truth! Cross my heart and hope to die."

Brian looked pensively back at the direction they had come from and at the store. "That's weird."

"Totally," Chris agreed.

"I don't know. That seems a bit far-fetched," Sam said.

"Well, you can believe what you want. I'm only

telling you what actually happened. You are more than welcome to go back there and find out for yourself," Chris said. He didn't say it maliciously, but he could feel himself getting heated, not out of anger but more so out of fear. He couldn't explain what had just happened and that made him afraid.

"No...no...I believe you," Sam said. "Besides, I'm not heading back there if you aren't going to go with me."

Chris was about to reply because he knew that Sam didn't believe him. He might have said it, but he didn't really believe it. Then his brother spoke up. "What are we going to do?" he asked.

"I'm not sure. If we see the hermit, I don't think any of us should be alone with him." Chris said.

"Yeah, that sounds good, but I meant, what are we going to do...as in right now?" Brian asked.

"Oh...uh...well, let's continue over to the park and see if the carnival is setting up yet," Chris said, taking a moment to shift gears since the subject had changed. At first, the thought of talking about something else irked him but then as he changed focus, even about something as mundane as where they were heading, he wasn't quite as creeped out as he had been just a moment before.

The park was just a small stretch of land to the east of the town. There was nothing there except for a couple of small pavilions and covered picnic tables. It was a pleasant spot for a Sunday afternoon picnic, where you could eat while lazily watching the cars drive down the highway. However, in all the summers and other times that Chris had visited, he had never seen anyone ever use the park, not even once. Even though Chris' mind was preoccupied with trying to comprehend the events at the store, it still surprised him to see people were actually at the park and lo and behold, putting up carnival rides. The carnival had arrived! In the back of Chris' thoughts, he had found it hard to believe they would really come to Stonemill. They never had before, so to see them there today was a pleasant surprise and he could feel his excitement rise. That was the real beauty of carnivals and local or state fairs–the possibilities of opportunity that came with them. Hope and opportunities for fun, experiences and memories, all very powerful things for the young and young at heart. So, it was no surprise that Chris quickly forgot the events of the morning as he watched the carnival being built right before his eyes. His mind drifted to how he would like to see Jessica here this weekend and maybe hang out with her.

Chapter Nine

The carnival was bigger than what Chris imagined it would be. There was no way the local inhabitants of the town would fill it but then again, there were plenty of little towns just like Stonemill, most of which were larger, in the surrounding areas and he was sure their residents would also come. It would probably be the most people this little town has seen in a while.

Now that the carnival was confirmed, Chris' thoughts turned to more urgent matters– the fact that they needed money. Sure, they were good for a dollar or two here or there. His mom left them a little money to get through the summer with. It wasn't much but it was good for a can of soda every now and then, like what they had gotten that morning.

Chris turned to Sam, who knew more of the townsfolk, and asked if he knew of anyone that would need chores done around their houses. Sam knew exactly what he was getting at because his thoughts were narrowing down on the same outcome…that they needed money to enjoy the carnival. Pretty soon, Sam came up with a list of names, some of which Chris and Brian recognized since they were church members who lived in town and on the surrounding farms. There were also some names they didn't recognize.

They didn't have much time and needed to get stuff done today and tomorrow morning, if they didn't collect enough cash today. They were supposed to meet the Darling sisters tomorrow around 6 PM, according to Brian. That was a great time during the summer because there would still be enough daylight left to enjoy, but they would also get to see all the neon and flashing lights of the carnival after dark. Chris was kicking himself, regretting they hadn't started doing odd jobs and collecting money sooner, in plenty of time for the "main event" this weekend. He honestly thought that the carnival wouldn't come and now he felt behind the power curve.

With the list of names, they went back into the heart of the town to canvas the area. Thankfully, being a small village and not a large town, it wouldn't take long to visit the different houses looking for work. They decided to start with the names of the people whom they all knew and went to church with. That surely wouldn't be nearly as much of a hard sell as compared to townsfolk they weren't familiar with. No matter how well-intentioned something or someone could be, when it's coming from an unknown, there's likely to be initial suspicion…and they just didn't have the time to waste.

No one answered the door at the first two homes they tried. Well–that marks Mrs. King and Mr. Johnson off the list. The stopped by Mr. and Mrs. Duren's house and they were home! Unfortunately, they didn't have anything for them to do. Mrs. Duren didn't want them to leave empty-handed so she gave them some cookies from the batch she had just made for her grandkids. She was always nice to them...she was always nice to everyone. The cookies were fantastic and appreciated, but would not pay for their fun night at the carnival.

The boys moved on to the next block and one by one, the names on the list dwindled. By mid-afternoon, they were getting a little frantic. With the big night fast approaching, they were afraid they wouldn't be able to really enjoy the carnival if they didn't have any cash to ride or play games. If the Darling girls were able to ride and they weren't, how embarrassing would that be?

By the afternoon, they ran out of names they all recognized and went on to the names that only Sam knew. Sure enough, that proved to be about as useful as a zit. Either no one was home, or they didn't have anything for the boys to do. Well, there went that idea like a candle flame in the wind.

"Now what?" Sam asked.

"I don't know. We walked all over town and nothing. I'm getting kind of tired. We may as well go home," Chris said, feeling dejected, which summed up the general mood of the small group.

"Shouldn't have bought those sodas this week," Brian said.

It was a calculated risk every time money was spent at this age. They didn't have the luxury of an allowance like Chris had heard of other kids getting. Nope–no allowance for these boys, so when they got money, it was a limited commodity. They had to be really careful about what they were going to do with it since they never knew when they'd be able to get more. It came either by kindness from their parents or other family members, or little jobs that would pop up from time to time, like mowing the neighbor's yard or some other random chore. However, it did teach them to be frugal. They had the money that mom left them, but Chris didn't want to blow it all this weekend. They still had a long summer left and who knew what else would come up? He knew that Aunt Christie and Uncle Bob didn't have any extra cash and were struggling to make ends meet, as well.

"Come on. Let's go," Chris said.

They trudged up the hill leading out of town and past the Catholic church. Father Bishop was outside and waved at the boys when he saw them.

"Well, it can't hurt to ask him," Chris said, thinking out loud.

Sam twisted his face up at Chris. "Are you sure?" he asked.

"Why not?" Chris asked.

"I don't know. I would have never thought to ask a church for money. It's usually the other way around, from what I hear," he said.

"Maybe, but we don't have a whole lot of options and it's better to know for sure," Chris said.

Sam agreed with this line of thinking and the boys walked over to Father Bishop. The priest was heading inside the church but when he saw them walking toward him, he stopped and waited.

"Hello, boys. How are you doing today?" he said cheerfully.

Chris answered and went into his spiel that he had given over a half dozen times already that day. "We are doing good, sir...uh...Father. Do you have any chores that need to be done around the church or around your house? The reason we ask is there's that carnival in town and we'd like to have a little extra money so we can go."

Father Bishop looked down at the boys, then shifted his gaze toward where the carnival would be held, though they couldn't see it from there. "Oh that's right. They are setting up today, aren't they?"

He then looked back at the boys, smiled and continued, "I remember when I was a boy. I loved it when the carnival came to the town I grew up in. There was always that sense of excitement. I think I can find something for you three to do."

"It's okay. We appr...wait...what?" Chris asked, surprised because this was the first affirmative response they had gotten all day.

"Yeah, come on in and follow me," he said and turned to go inside the church.

The boys followed and the refreshing cool air welcomed them as they came through the door. "Hmm...let's see. You two," as he pointed to Sam and Brian, "I would like for you to do dust the pews and the pulpit. Can you do that?"

"Sure!" they both said simultaneously.

Father Bishop got out the cleaning supplies and

handed them to the boys to get started. "And you," pointing to Chris, "I'd like you to vacuum the sanctuary and foyer."

The boys went to work. The church was already meticulously clean, but the boys put just as much effort into it as if it were an old, dirty house that needed a deep cleaning. Once they had finished those chores, Father Bishop directed them to other things he wanted them to do. The jobs weren't hard because like it was stated before, Father Bishop kept his house in order. The last thing that he wanted the boys to do was to help move some furniture and boxes in the basement. It seemed like some of the items hadn't been moved in years and had a coat of dust that seemed almost blasphemous when compared to the level of cleanliness everywhere else in the church.

"All right, boys," Father Bishop spoke, "I'm trying to clear the area down here for future gatherings and I'm so glad you all are here to help me. I don't think I would be able to tackle this on my own."

They commenced to moving in the largest room. They shifted, tilted, lifted, scooted and reorganized boxes, statues, and other decor. There were two storage rooms on either side of the main room that needed organization, as well. It took a couple of hours but eventually, the place was in order and even though the two storage rooms were full, they weren't haphazardly disorganized. Father Bishop could now easily maneuver and find what he needed when he needed it. They made considerable room in the main area of the basement, as well.

After they were done, the father went back upstairs and came back holding enough cups of water, one for each of them. After a period of heavy activity or work, there was always a time to relax and reflect on the accomplishment, and this was one of those times. They enjoyed the cold water while looking over what they had finished in momentary silence and satisfaction.

Father Bishop broke the silence. "That was great, boys. That would have taken me forever. Thank you."

Chris, too tired to think, just nodded along with the two other boys. A few moments later, they all left the basement together and Father Bishop followed them out the front door.

"Well, let's see," he said to the boys as he pulled out his wallet and opened it. He looked up into the air as if he was doing mental calculations and then, as if coming to a decision, he shrugged, smiled and looked back at the boys. He pulled three crisp ten-dollar bills from the old wallet and handed them out, one to each to them.

Chris hadn't expected this. He looked down at the ten-dollar bill in his hand just to make sure it wasn't fake, then looked at the priest. "Are you sure?"

Chris was expecting maybe five bucks. Anything would have been nice, and they had worked pretty hard, especially in the basement, but he didn't expect this. The other boys were thinking the same thing, but Brian stuffed the ten in his pants pocket. Sam shared Chris' look of uncertainty.

Noticing the boys' apprehension, Father Bishop

spoke, "Yeah, I am. You boys did a good job, didn't complain, nor did you waste time. You also saved me a lot of time and trouble had I done all that on my own. Besides, that's all I have on me and don't have change. It's just money and I was young once, too. Go enjoy the carnival but be careful."

"Thanks," Chris said, still in amazement at the good fortune that had befallen them.

Sam looked at Chris and when he realized it was all good, he followed Brian and stuffed the bill into his pocket. They all looked at Father Bishop in a new light all of a sudden. He had always seemed nice before but now, it was like seeing someone you are used to seeing after they did something drastic to change their appearance. Sometimes you reclassify someone in your mind based on new actions versus what you had previously thought about them. The boys snapped out of it rather quickly, though, to avoid awkwardness.

Father Bishop turned and went back inside, leaving them out front.

"Wow," Chris managed to say. "Ten dollars."

"Mom's going to make us give it back. I just know it," Sam said.

"No, she won't," Brian said, then after a moment added, "We don't have to tell her."

"I don't know," Sam said.

"We'll tell her the truth. We did chores for people in town and they paid us," Chris said.

"I know...but it just seems too good to be true. Just waiting for that other shoe to drop," Sam said.

"Oh, it will be fine," Chris said. "Besides, we won't have to ask for money now. We have more than enough for admission and a few rides. We'll even have enough for a soda and maybe a slice of pizza."

They changed their thoughts to what tomorrow would bring as they left the Catholic church and continued home. Chris thought to himself, "Heck, I may even have enough to pay for Jessica to ride a couple of rides or buy her a soft drink." It wasn't a date, he knew, but he allowed himself to let his mind wander over in secret hopes. If he spoke those thoughts out loud, his brother would never let him live it down, even though he had an inkling that Brian might be having those same thoughts about Erin. Chris felt good; he had money to cover costs, Jessica was now single, and opportunities felt promising. Who knew what could happen? He didn't know, but he was certainly looking forward to finding out.

Halfway back to the house, Chris' thoughts changed as he reflected over the day's events. It had been a day of extremes, from feelings of the unbelievably strange to feelings of being unbelievably blessed. This made him start thinking about Ol' Ned again. It was all so strange–the way he just disappeared and then Mrs. Willing acting as if nothing happened. Chris noticed that little feeling of anxiety creep back up into the depths of his body, which happened every time he thought of Ol' Ned lately. He had always heard, "Trust your gut" but he never really knew what that meant. He wondered if this feeling he was having was what that phrase referred to.

"You okay?" Brian asked.

"Yeah. Why?" Chris replied.

"You just seemed to just stop suddenly. Wanna talk about it?"

"No," Chris said, as he looked back at his brother and saw the look of concern in his face. "Everything's fine. I was just thinking over the day."

"Yeah, I'm kind of tired, too," Brian said. He thought Chris meant he was thinking about all the work they had done earlier and while that was partly true, it didn't cover the depth or breadth of what was rolling through Chris' mind. Chris knew that Brian missed his mark, but didn't elaborate to correct his brother.

"Yeah, let's get home. I think I am ready to get this day over with," was all Chris said.

Chapter Ten

Friday night came and went. The excitement and anticipation for Saturday evening caused Chris to wake up early...well, early for him. He went downstairs and into the kitchen where his Aunt Christie greeted him. His Uncle Bob was out at the barn down the road, following his schedule of feeding his livestock, which included only four cows, three horses and a couple of pigs. One of the cows died last year during a freak lightning storm but nothing went to waste here, and it provided good eating.

"How'd you sleep?" his aunt asked.

"With my eyes closed," came his reply.

"Hardy, har, har," she said in feigned amusement.

"No–I slept alright," Chris said. "You?"

"I slept okay, but I did have some bad dreams that woke me up," Aunt Christie said.

"Really? What were they?"

"I can't really remember...just that they were odd, like something was coming and I didn't like it. It took me forever to get back to sleep."

"Oh, that stinks," Chris said.

"You looking forward to tonight?" she asked.

Chris played it cool. "Oh yeah. I'm sure we'll have a good time." He thought to himself, "How much did I let on about going to the carnival?" Aunt Christie wasn't dumb, and she knew that Chris had had his eye on Jessica from time to time. She also knew that Brian and Sam were going to meet Erin there, so it wasn't hard to guess that Jessica would probably be there, too.

"I'm sure you will," she said, smiling as if thinking of an inside joke that Chris didn't get or one that he refused to pay any attention to.

"Are you and Uncle Bob going?" Chris asked.

"Oh, no. We'll probably just drop you all off. But then again, if we do stay, we may just stick around for an ice cream cone or something."

"That will be good," Chris said, then changing the subject, asked "You know that Catholic priest in town?"

"No, not really. I hear he is a real nice guy. He hasn't been here that long, just a couple years. Well...let me think," she said, then added a few seconds later, "No, he's been here longer than a couple years, but it hasn't been too, terribly long."

"Yeah, he gave us some work yesterday and paid us really well for it," Chris said. Chris knew that Sam was worried what his parents would say but Chris didn't think that Aunt Christie would care as long as it was earned. He was right–she didn't mind at all. "Well, that was very nice of him," she said.

"We certainly didn't expect it."

Brian and Sam came into the kitchen shortly thereafter and they all ate a bowl of oatmeal. It wasn't as good as the homemade buttermilk biscuits that Aunt Christie was a master at making, but it served its purpose and wasn't too bad. Chris stood up from the table and noticed the soreness in his muscles from all the work they did yesterday, but it felt good as a reminder of their accomplishment.

Aunt Christie had the radio playing, which was a usual custom in the household. She liked to listen to the music and sometimes, she would turn it to the church broadcasts and listen to sermons from time to time. It was an older radio, with knobs you had to turn in order to tune in to the desired radio station frequency. It sat on the windowsill and right now, a local news program was on the air. A meteorologist came on and gave the forecast for today and the next couple of days.

"...Tonight, scattered showers with a chance of thunderstorms, being..."

Chris didn't listen to it all and only in passing, but long enough to whisper a prayer that it didn't rain tonight. He had things to do and didn't want it to get ruined on the account of weather. Quickly, his focus changed and he thought of Jessica. Yep–he didn't want anything to ruin the chance to hang out with her. He smiled as he went back upstairs to take a shower and get ready for the day...more importantly, to get ready for the evening.

It didn't take long to get ready and as time goes, it was a case of "hurry up and wait," as time slowed to a crawl as it had seemed to do all week, anticipating the carnival. But no matter how slowly time sometimes seems to pass, it does pass and, in many cases, it eventually tends to sneak up like a surprise attack that you had forewarning about, but weren't paying particular attention to. It's almost like watching weeds grow–then you take your eyes off and realize they grew three inches in the time that you looked away.

Aunt Christie and Uncle Bob gave them a ride to town and dropped them off in the parking area where the traveling carnival had set up. It had grown significantly since yesterday. Rides were everywhere and surprisingly, the carnival was full of people. The population of Stonemill swelled momentarily, probably two to three times its normal size.

Chris jumped out of the bed of the truck and made the move quickly to the ticket booth but then stopped, went back to the cab of the truck, and thanked his aunt and uncle for the ride.

"Ok, boys, we will be back around 9 PM," his aunt said "And we will meet you right here."

"Okay," they replied.

"Tell me what time and where we are meeting," she instantly said.

"Right here at 9 PM," Chris said.

"Great. Have a good time!" she said.

Chris stepped back from the window and watched them leave, the dust from the parking area kicking up as they rolled on. He could feel Brian and Sam getting antsy beside him. They were ready to go on into the heart of the carnival. It wasn't cordoned off. Anyone could come and go but if one wanted to ride the rides, they had to go to one of the ticket booths that were scattered throughout, to pay for tickets.

"Where are we meeting Erin and Jessica?" Chris asked.

"At the entrance..." Brian answered, but then trailed off as he realized there were no dedicated entrances. "Uh...well...I'm sure we'll run into them."

They were saved from looking when only a moment later, they heard Erin call out, "Hey guys!"

The boys turned and saw Erin running toward them. Chris looked beyond Erin to search for Jessica but didn't see her. He only saw Erin's parents driving off from where they dropped her off. "Well, that's a bummer," he thought. She should have been here with Erin, from what he understood.

"Hey, Erin," both Brian and Sam greeted her. Chris thought that both of them probably had a crush on her, but never delved into the subject because he didn't want to shed light on his own thoughts about the Darling sisters, namely Jessica. Chris couldn't contain his curiosity and had to ask. "Where's Jessica?"

"Oh, she'll be here in a little bit with her boyfriend," she said.

"Oh." Chris immediately felt the sinking feeling in his stomach of best laid plans going down in flames, like an old ship getting bashed on a rocky shore and going down during a storm. He was seriously surprised at the news, but then quickly steeled himself. He didn't want to give anything away to the group about the turmoil that he was fighting inside. "Why did I ever think she might be interested in me? So stupid…" he thought to himself. "I should have never given it any energy…" as well as a few other thoughts, generally berating himself for being a fool.

None of the other group noticed and Erin continued with her explanation, "Yeah, they patched things up last night and they are going on a 'date' here, but my parents still want her to hang out with us in the group so she can keep an eye on me," she said while rolling her eyes and using her fingers as quotation marks around the word "date." She showed some disdain about her parents thinking she needed her sister to look after her.

The news didn't make the situation any better for Chris. "Oh, great," he thought to himself. "I'm gonna have my nose rubbed into it just like a puppy that made an accident on the carpet." And just like that, he didn't want to be at the carnival any longer. Nothing ever turns out as good or as bad as you expect it to be, this situation being the former.

"They should be here any minute. He was picking her up from the house as we were leaving," Erin continued. Chris' sense of dread just got worse with every word that dripped from her mouth. And sure enough, as if on cue, they saw Jessica and her boyfriend pull into the parking area in a flashy, brand-new, electric-blue truck. Chris looked over at the truck as the driver revved the engine for show. He immediately did mental calculations and came to the conclusion that no one he was related to could afford something like that. He certainly wouldn't have been able to buy something like that, but then again, he couldn't even drive by himself yet. Even when he could, he knew that a vehicle of that caliber wasn't in the cards for him, at least not anytime soon. With what Jessica had already told him about this guy, coupled with how he whipped into the parking lot, showing off, Chris decidedly didn't like him.

Chris sighed and resigned himself to the coming evening, suppressing his emotions to the point of feeling numb, which made him feel cool and reserved. A moment later, Jessica walked up and said "Hello" and introduced the guy as Brandon. Brandon looked like a football jock and likely the kind of guy that would have worn his letterman jacket tonight if it wasn't summer. He was taller than Chris and had jet-black hair. He was thin with a muscular build that looked more like it was from gym work than farm work. Yup–Chris didn't like him.

Chris just nodded as Jessica introduced the gang to Brandon, who from Chris' point of view, didn't appear to care or pay attention to. Jessica turned to her sister Erin and said, "Hey, I know you are going to be okay hanging out with these guys. Do you mind if Brandon and I go do our own thing? I know mom wanted us to hang out together but there's a lot to do here and we may not want to do the..."

"Yeah...whatever. That's fine," Erin cut her off. "Come on, guys. Let's go," she said to Brian and Sam, as she ran toward the ticket booth. She didn't really care what her sister did. She was in a hurry to go enjoy the carnival. The sudden movement surprised everyone. Brian and Sam quickly followed as they ran after her, leaving Chris behind with Jessica and Brandon looking at each other, which made the moment even more awkward. But it was only awkward for Chris, as it seemed that Jessica and Brandon were more caught up with each other than anyone else. Chris again just nodded and turned to follow, but quickly fell behind because Erin and the rest of gang were already off into the depths of the carnival. Behind him, Jessica and Brandon melted away into another direction, leaving him alone. Again, nothing ever seems to turn out quite like you expect. Chris didn't know which was worse, having his nose rubbed into it or being alone, surrounded by people he didn't know.

"Man, I just wanna go home. I wish I had never come here this summer," Chris said aloud, but quietly, to himself. He thought of his friend Mike back home in Florida, who by now, was probably neck deep in the chlorinated water of his family pool, the one that Chris could have enjoyed had he been able to stay home this summer. Oh well…nothing he could do about it. He was here now, so might as well enjoy what he could. He trudged up to the ticket booth and got in line, which had lengthened since Erin, Brian and Sam got their tickets. Looking over the crowd for his brother, he didn't see him. "That punk! He totally left me behind," Chris thought to himself. The line went quickly and finally Chris got up to the window, which had a gap through which to speak and exchange tickets and money, just above the counter. Behind the glass was a lady with fiery red hair and heavy makeup who was smacking her gum and looked bored to tears and like she was just waiting for her next smoke break.

"What will it be?" she asked Chris in a tone that matched her expression as if to imply, "Hurry up, kid; you're bothering me."

Chris quickly looked over the prices and decided to go with the wristband, which was a little pricier than the individual tickets but allowed the wearer to ride as many rides as they wanted. It didn't help at all for the games or food though, as you still had to fork over money at the individual booths. He gave the crotchety-appearing lady his money, pocketed the change and stuck his wrist through the window slot so she could attach the flimsy, neon-orange, paper wristband.

"Have fun," she said, then looked over Chris' shoulder at the next customer. Chris moved away and headed into the carnival. It was already crowded and it seemed to be getting more so. He didn't get too far from the booth when Brian materialized, walking beside him.

"Where'd you come from?" Chris asked. "I thought y'all left me behind."

"I wouldn't leave you behind. You wouldn't leave me behind," Brian said.

For a moment, Chris felt good that they were brothers. But then again, he always felt good they were brothers. Of course, they sometimes had their squabbles, but they always had each other's back and knew they could count on one another. But tonight, he felt crummy and was glad that his brother waited so that he wouldn't be alone.

"Thanks," he said.

"Sam and Erin ran ahead. I told them to wait up, but they were gone, so...whatever. I saw a really cool ride over that way," Brian said, indicating a direction a couple of rows over. Chris smiled and said "Sure" then noticed that Brian also got the wristband. "We can ride all the rides. One thing's for sure, though, I want to ride the Ferris wheel. I want to see how everything looks from above."

And then, the night didn't seem so bad after all. Chris and his brother had a good time, running from event to event, almost getting sick on a couple of rides. Chris was glad that he skipped dinner with the intention of getting something to eat at the carnival. He was sure he would have upchucked had his stomach been full. He was impressed with what the traveling carnival had to offer. It was one of the better ones he had ever been to. It was just surprising that it was here, of all places.

After an hour went by, both Chris and Brian started to get hungry, so they grabbed a couple of slices of pizza and a soda from one of the food booths, and downed it all pretty quickly. They hadn't seen Sam, Erin or even Jessica and Brandon in the past hour, which was almost surprising. It was a nice-sized carnival but not so big that you wouldn't run into someone. Then again, with the fun houses and other mini-attractions, they could have easily missed each other in passing.

They walked down one of the aisles and came

across a tent that had a palm reader sign outside. It had a worn-out looking picture of a hand and fading letters that read, "Madame Zara's Fortune Telling," with smaller letters telling passersby to inquire within.

"Hey, let's go get our fortunes read!" Brian said.

"Outlook does not look good," Chris thought to himself, as he was thinking about his summer experiences so far, which had been weird and uncertain. Chris also didn't want to waste his money, "Nah, man…that's a waste. All she is going to tell you are things you want to hear," Chris said.

"What's wrong with that?" Brian asked, jokingly. "But seriously, I want to hear what she has to say."

"Ok…fine…waste your money if you want to. I am not doing it, but I'll go in with you," Chris said.

They entered the tent; it was larger than it appeared from the outside, with a little corridor that opened into a large room. It was pretty dark inside, with low lighting. At the center of the room was a table and behind the table sat a lady wearing long, flowing robes with white, flowing hair. She had a weathered look about her; she had a dark tan and looked almost grandmotherly. The table was covered with a silky, dark blue tablecloth, and there was a crystal ball sitting on one side of it. The lady looked up at the boys as they entered, then stood up to gesture "Welcome," as well as guide them to the seats before her.

"Come in. Come in, boys. Have a seat and let Madame Zara tell you your future," she greeted them in a sultry, yet booming voice.

Brian eagerly entered the room from the corridor and sat down at the table. Chris reluctantly followed and sat down beside his brother in one of the two seats that were opposite the old lady. She spoke with a theatrical flair as she went into her spiel and sat down in her own chair.

"Welcome to Madame Zara's Fortune Telling. I will tell you your future–the good, the bad and whatever else the spirits tell me."

"How hokey," Chris thought to himself. He had to try very hard to keep a straight face so it wouldn't betray his thoughts. It's one thing to think things; it's another to let your thoughts be known and hurt others. Chris was very cognizant of that. He didn't want to make the lady feel bad, even though he knew it was all an act.

"Give me your hand, young man, and let the fates tell me of your future. Madame Zara knows all...sees all," the lady said, as she lifted her hand up to her forehead, which to Chris, made it look like she had a headache but really, it was just more theatrics. Seriously, who refers to herself in third person? Madame Zara reached across the table and took Brian's hand, who willingly offered it. She then immediately recoiled, as if bitten by a snake, and her face contorted from a smile to a troubled look. She quickly regained composure as she played it off. Chris noticed and asked if everything was okay.

"Why, yes child. Everything is fine...I just...wasn't expec..." she didn't finish the sentence and trailed off, as if she realized that she was still in front of customers and had to get back into character. "Yes.

Everything is fine," she said with flair, "I just wasn't expecting the electrical personalities of you two young men this evening."

Even though she had regained her façade, Chris thought he could sense a little hesitation on her part as she looked at them. "Yes, let me look at the crystal ball and invoke the power of the spirits to whisper to Madame Zara!"

She pulled the crystal ball to the center of the table and moved her hands in swirling motions all around it. She then gazed deeply into it, looking at, well…Chris could only guess.

"This is interesting…very interesting," she said in her Madame Zara voice. Then her demeanor changed and as she continued examining the crystal ball, her face took on a look of heavy concentration. The act of Madame Zara fell away, as she spoke plainly in a normal conversational tone and no longer in an overdramatic manner. "This is uh…interesting…and a bit concerning, boys," she said as she looked up at Brian and Chris.

"What are you boys into?" she asked, with all pretenses of Madame Zara gone.

"What do you mean?" Chris asked.

Chapter Eleven

"I don't know," she said, "But something isn't quite right, here. I see a lot of people come through that tent door and I've never seen anything quite like this," she said. Her voice took on a concerned tone as she looked between the boys and the crystal ball before her.

"What do you see?" Brian asked.

"It's very dark. Let me start by saying that fortune telling isn't exact. It's mostly hints and possibilities but there is a very...dark future here. It's showing me that you are on a dangerous path. It's giving me goosebumps," she said, shivering. She then squinted as she peered further into the crystal ball. She suddenly popped her head back up and looked straight at the boys, then around them, as if she were looking at something they couldn't see and she couldn't understand. Her face took on a suspicious expression at whatever she saw and, in that moment, she made up her mind. "Actually, I want you boys out of my tent," she said quietly, almost whispering.

"What?!" Chris said surprisedly, almost bordering on being flabbergasted.

"The reading is free. I don't want your money. Whatever you're involved with, I don't want any part of it. I just want you boys out of here," she said.

By this time, all pretenses of "Madame Zara" were long gone, replaced by a stern, apparently frightened lady telling them to leave her tent without offering any explanation. The whole experience unexpectedly went from being comical to being grave really quickly. Chris tried to neutralize the situation and started, "Listen Ma'am, we have no..."

But Madame Zara, or whatever her real name was, interrupted, "I don't want to hear it. I seriously just want you both to leave. I do not want to be a part of this."

Whatever she saw caused so much distress that she got up from the table and began to leave through a fold in the back of the tent. She did pause for a moment to look back, then shook her head and disappeared.

The boys were left stunned as they awkwardly stood up and found their way out the front of the tent. They didn't speak to each other for a few minutes, as each boy was trying to process what had just taken place.

Finally, Brian broke that silence as they stood in front of the tent, "Well, that was...unexpected," trying to find the right word but not finding anything to fit.

Chris grunted in agreement, as there was really nothing to say. It was bizarre and creepy, thought Chris. They stood for a bit longer in silence. Chris realized they couldn't stand in front of the tent all night so finally spoke up. "Well, we may as well get the Ferris wheel out of the way."

His excitement regarding the carnival and all its

rides had seriously waned. "What a roller coaster ride of emotions this evening has been (pun intended)," he thought to himself. Maybe it was all part of the old lady's act, to create stories of intrigue. This was one of the many thoughts bouncing around in his mind, trying to make sense of it all, but really–who was he kidding? He didn't believe that...not one little bit. That lady was genuinely scared, like being surprised by a water moccasin rearing to strike, then jumping back to give it a wide berth.

Brian agreed, so they headed toward the wheel that towered over the whole carnival like a mountain that overlooked a village. By this time, the sun had gone down, and the lights of the carnival were bright and captivating, as most people couldn't resist the excitement of all the blinking and glowing neon lights. When the boys reached the wheel, they showed the attendant their wrist bands, who then allowed them on the platform. The next seat arrived, and it only took a few seconds for the previous occupants to depart. Chris and Brian got into the seat, which was really just a bench that looked precariously attached to the wheel. Another attendant came over and lowered the seat's restraint bar over Chris and Brian's laps to keep them in place. It didn't seem all that secure, as there was plenty of room for them to move around in the seat, but it did provide something for them to hold onto. The attendant went back to the control pedestal and a moment later, their seat lurched forward as music started to play. The wheel turned, lifting Chris and Brian higher and higher. The seat canted back a little as it freed the platform and it felt pretty rickety; any movement caused the seat to rock as it balanced to right itself. It was cool seeing the land from the heights as they moved up. It's funny how everything looks different when you see it from a different vantage point. They made a few revolutions, with the attendant stopping every so often to let others off and on the ride. On the last rotation, Chris and Brian were stopped momentarily on the top while far below, the seat inhabitants exchanged. They could see everything from up here. They looked over the carnival ground and even though the sun had set, the lights were bright enough that Chris noticed he could still make out the people below. He looked more closely and thought he saw Sam and Erin heading down one of the carnival corridors by the food. He looked to the left and saw Jessica and Brandon on the other side of the carnival. Ugh. He quickly looked away. Off in the far distance, he saw a storm brewing with lightning flashes. He momentarily thought, "That will be here before we know it." Storms in southern Illinois did that. They would pop up seemingly out of nowhere and move rapidly.

He looked down each corridor of booths and other rides in front of Brian and him. "Wait–it couldn't be. Was that Ol' Ned?" He squinted, trying to get a better look, and sure enough, it was. "What's he doing here?" Chris asked himself. As if on cue, Ol' Ned looked up and although he was on the other side of the carnival, Chris knew that he was looking straight at him. Ol' Ned smiled, and Chris could see his teeth. Chris noticed that Mrs. Willing, the store clerk, was in front of Ol' Ned. From Chris' point of view, it looked like they were either together or he was following her. Something about what he was looking at just didn't feel right. Ol' Ned's smile seemed to get wider, if that was possible. Of course, Chris thought his eyes could have been playing tricks on him, given the low light and distance between them. Whatever the case, he felt that sense of warning stir deep within his gut again. With everything going on this week, he had almost forgotten that feeling; he hadn't had that since the last time he saw Ol' Ned. He also felt compelled to go see if Mrs. Willing was okay.

"Do you see Ol' Ned over there?" Chris asked his brother.

His brother was looking over the side in another direction and looked to where Chris indicated. He squinted as his eyes moved over the area.

"No, I don't...Oh, there he is," he replied "Strange...would have never thought of him as the carnival type. Ya know, him being a hermit and all."

"I think there are a lot of things strange about that old man," Chris thought to himself. Chris looked beyond the hermit, at the night sky over the hill overlooking Stonemill and the carnival. It was darkening and the storm looked to be moving closer as they heard distant rumbling from the thunder. He looked back down and Ol' Ned was nowhere to be seen–neither was Mrs. Willing.

A moment later, the wheel lurched forward again to begin its descent to the platform below. As soon they reached the bottom and the attendant raised the protective bar, Chris hurriedly jumped out of the car and exited the back side of the ride.

"Come on. We have to hurry," Chris said, as he

grabbed his brother to make sure he didn't lose him in the rush.

"What are you talking about and what are you doing?" Brian asked as he was being half-dragged.

"It's the store lady, Mrs. Willing. I think she's in trouble," Chris replied, not slowing down. He dodged bodies as he navigated through the crowd, still holding onto Brian.

"Why do you..."

Chris didn't give Brian a chance to finish, as he anticipated the question that was coming. "I don't know. It's just a feeling. I have to check it out."

"Okay. Fine. Just let me go," Brian said.

Chris looked down to where he had a hold of his brother and let go. "Sorry. I just don't want to lose you," Chris said.

"Don't worry...I don't want to be lost," Brian said in a half-sarcastic tone, and ran alongside him.

They ran to the area he had last seen the hermit and Mrs. Willing, but they weren't there. Chris started searching the side alleys and areas between booths that led to other corridors. He didn't know why, but he started feeling frantic as he searched. It was the same feeling one would get while searching for a missing, last piece of 1000-piece jigsaw puzzle–everything hinged on finding that last piece. It just had to be there. They just had to be there. He turned around to say something to Brian, but he was gone. The frantic feeling went to max level. Chris could feel the blood starting to pound in his face near his eyes as he almost gave way to panic. He was beginning to feel faint.

"Brian!" he screamed, running back from where they had come and where he last saw him. "Brian!"

A feeling of despair was building in Chris' young mind when he heard, "Over here!"

It was Brian, thank goodness. He had gone down one of the alleys and was in another corridor, paralleling Chris' own position. Immediate relief swept through Chris as he pushed through on wobbly legs to grab Brian.

"I'm not letting you go this time," Chris said, as he grabbed Brian's shoulder. "You scared me! I thought you were gone."

Normally, the word "gone" would have meant something momentarily and wouldn't have been a big deal...but something about tonight was different. The carnival was larger than expected–not so large that they wouldn't have found each other eventually–but with the appearance of Ol' Ned...well, that changed things. They also hadn't seen Sam, Erin or Jessica and her boyfriend since they split up earlier that evening. That was another worrisome thought that began to grow in Chris' mind.

"Oh, come on, man. I was right here," Brian replied, slightly annoyed. "I thought we could cover more area by spreading out a little."

Chris stopped and looked at his brother to make sure what he said would sink in, but let it go. "Brian, it was a good idea, but I think we should stick together. Something feels really wrong about this whole evening."

"Okay," Brian said. "I'll stick to you like glue."

The rumble from thunder became more noticeable. Chris noticed other carnival-goers looking up, as if trying to gauge whether the storm was heading their way or not. It wasn't cause for concern yet, but it soon could be. Since most of the crowd were farmers or farmers' family members, they always kept an eye on the weather.

"Hey! Over there!" Brian said while Chris was looking the other way. Chris turned his gaze to where his brother indicated and saw Ol' Ned and Mrs. Willing way on the other end of the corridor. They turned next to a booth at the far end, disappearing from sight. On that side of the carnival, there was just wilderness and fields beyond. Chris couldn't see many people venturing out that way. He had to find out where they had gone, so started heading that direction with Brian running closely beside him. He made sure that Brian was always in his view as they moved. They weren't as fast that way, but that didn't matter as much as their safety.

As they got halfway down the corridor, they heard their names being called from behind. This irritated Chris because he was on a mission and a distraction was frustrating. Just a few more moments and they would have been at the last spot they had seen Ol' Ned and Mrs. Willing. Brian and Chris turned to find Sam and Erin waving and calling them. They were roughly the same distance from them as they were from the spot they were heading to. To go back would mean giving up on checking on Mrs. Willing and seeing what Ol' Ned was up to, but continuing forward might mean losing Sam and Erin again. Chris looked down at his watch and saw the time. It was currently 8:40 PM and his aunt and uncle would be there soon to pick them up. He had to make a choice and he had to make it fast. He turned toward Brian and said, "Look–I know I said we need to stick together but we don't have the time. We can't lose those two, so I need you to run back and get them to stay put. I'm going to run on ahead to see where Ol' Ned and Mrs. Willing went."

"That's not a good idea," Brian said. "I agree there are some weird things going on and like you said earlier, splitting up isn't a good idea."

"I know. But listen…you run back and then keep an eye on me. I won't leave this corridor. Once I see what happened, I will be coming back," Chris said.

Brian thought about it a moment, "Fine. But I still don't like it."

The thunder overhead was getting closer by the minute, along with the lightning. If Chris had more time, he would have been mesmerized by the show in the clouds. He had always been fascinated by lightning and the way it made the clouds flash like strobe lights. The storm that was coming looked like it was gaining in ferocity and closing in quickly, by looking at the tempo of flashes. The glow from the flashes also silhouetted and highlighted the growing storm clouds. It was obvious it was coming and rides started shutting down. Ride attendants corralled people off and away from the different structures.

With many of the rides towering above nearby trees and all of them being constructed of metal, they were prime targets for lighting.

The boys split up. Brian ran back to Sam and Erin as Chris ran the other way, toward the end of the corridor. When he had almost reached the end, Chris passed a dark alley between two booths where he heard a familiar voice, prompting him to stop.

"Let go of me!"

"Oh, come on," Chris heard another voice say, "You know you want to. No need to act like a baby."

"No, I don't! Let me go!" Jessica said as she twisted free from Brandon, who was holding her arm. She ran out of the shadow that enveloped the alley and into the corridor. She saw Chris and walked toward him. Now, Chris was really torn between seeing what happened to Ol' Ned and Mrs. Willing and helping Jessica. But, she really looked like she needed help now, so he waited for her to catch up. Brandon emerged from the alley and shouted, "Hey! Wait up!"

She didn't slow and Brandon grabbed after her again.

"We are done," she said.

Chapter Twelve

"You don't get to tell me when we're done," he said with the look of a spoiled man-child who was used to getting his way. He successfully grabbed her shoulders and turned her around, not seeing Chris and not really paying attention to anyone else, for that matter. "Who do you think you are?" he half-shouted at her. Based off what Chris had seen so far, Brandon had a horrible sense of entitlement and treated everything and everybody like they were his playthings, including Jessica.

By this time, with the storm approaching, there weren't many people around to witness Brandon's behavior, other than Chris. Brandon was bigger and probably much stronger than he was, but he couldn't allow what he was seeing unfold in front of him. His dad, even though he wasn't around much, had at least taught him that much. He stepped forward as he mustered the courage to say something.

"Hey! Let her go," Chris said, trying to sound brave. Inside, he could feel the adrenaline start to rise and along with it, the anxiety about possible outcomes. Still holding onto Jessica by the arm, Brandon looked at Chris, noticing him for the first time. "Oh yeah? "What are you gonna to do about it?"

Thunder rolled overhead and Chris anticipated a

fight. "This is gonna hurt. Oh well…let's get this over with," he thought to himself, as he stepped forward. He stopped when he heard a voice behind him.

"Don't you mean 'what are we going to do about it?'" he heard his brother say. Chris quickly looked over his shoulder to see Brian, Sam and Erin walk up behind him. Relief was immediate for Chris, but they weren't out of danger. Who knew how far this guy would go?

"Let go of my sister, you creep," Erin said.

Sam and Brian balled up their fists, ready to fight. Sure, they were younger–Brian being eleven and Sam being thirteen–but fighting three boys and a sister while holding on to Jessica didn't seem like such a good idea to Brandon. He had his image and reputation to uphold, after all. Brandon let Jessica go and pushed her away. "Whatever. You don't know what you're missing," he said.

"You are such a jerk. I can't believe I gave you a second chance. I thought it might have been me…but no, it's all you. You're…just a jerk!" Jessica said. She wanted to say something worse, but she had manners.

Brandon's eyes narrowed at the accusation and replied, "Yeah, whatever, bi…"

However, Brandon either didn't finish what he was about to say, or the group couldn't hear it because lighting struck a nearby ride, causing them all to jump. It was so loud and startling that for a few moments, they didn't know whether they, themselves had been struck. The thunderclap that immediately followed deafened them while the white-hot bolt of lightning caused those looking toward it to go temporarily blind. It took a few moments to recover. Everyone in the corridor besides their group either ran for cover or decided it was time to leave. Brandon had already started to walk alone to the parking lot, not necessarily in a hurry but obviously not interested in sticking around, either. The group all looked around at each other as their eyesight returned, with Jessica finally breaking the silence.

"Thanks," she said.

"What happened?" Erin asked.

"Oh, he started getting a little too frisky and wouldn't take 'no' for an answer," Jessica said. "Like he felt that since he paid for everything, he should get something in return. I feel so stupid."

"It's okay," Chris said, trying to think of something but coming up with nothing to really help.

"I'm glad he backed down. I thought we were going to get beat up there for a second," Brian said.

Chris smiled because that's exactly what he had been thinking, as well. Thank God for small wonders. "Me too. I thought we were goners," Sam said.

"What are you guys talking about?" Erin said, "We totally had the numbers."

"Well...glad we didn't have to find out," Brian replied.

Brian and Chris looked at each other and volumes of thanks, relief and understanding passed between them in a way that only occurred between close siblings. "I'm glad you guys showed up," Chris said "How did you know to come?"

"I got to them as quick as I could and when we looked back, we saw you stop to look at something. We couldn't tell what it was, so we decided to come. Then we saw Jessica and started running because we figured there was a problem," Brian said.

The group carefully walked toward the parking lot as the wind picked up. Brian hung back a bit with Chris. "So, I guess we won't know what the deal was with Mrs. Willing and Ol' Ned."

Chris sighed and said, "I guess not. I hope she is okay. I mean…it was weird, right? I'm not crazy, am I?"

"I don't think you are. I mean…I didn't hear or see Mrs. Willing acting like she didn't remember Ol' Ned being at the store, but I believe you," Brian said.

"I still want to go look really quick," Chris said.

As Chris was about to excuse himself, Sam and Erin grabbed and held each other's hand, right in front of them all. Chris looked at his brother to see his reaction. He picked up on a momentary flash of something that he couldn't quantify, but it came and went quickly. Brian saw his brother watching him, so knew what his face had given away. He gave a little shrug and a half-hearted smile. Chris put his arm around Brian's shoulders, brought him in for a side hug and spoke only loud enough for Brian to hear. "Eh, I'm sure it's all fine. Let's get out of here," Chris said.

The wind continued and before they got to the parking area, the rain came, and boy was it a downpour. They sought shelter under a small awning on one of the booths. It wasn't much of a shelter, as it wasn't much of a roof, but it did buffet the wind coming in from the side to some extent. The carnival was emptying quickly as the crowds returned to their vehicles and left the area. All the carnival lights and rides were still powered on, which only made it seem more deserted. The small group was drenched by the time Jessica and Erin's parents arrived. It was about five minutes before 9 PM. "Crazy," thought Chris, "that so much can happen in a short amount of time." Erin and Sam hugged each other. Jessica took a step forward to leave, but then came back and hugged Chris and said, "Thanks again."

This caught Chris off-guard and he sputtered a reply he wasn't prepared for, "Oh... uh...sure...anytime...my pleasu..."

Jessica smiled, "See you tomorrow at church?"

"Uh...yeah. I'll be there."

"See you then."

The girls then ran together, cringing with their hands over their heads, trying to protect themselves from the rain. This seemed kind of funny to Chris since they were already soaked to the bone. They got into their parents' car and left.

Immediately, Brian turned on Sam. "What happened? You just left us...and what the heck? You and Erin are an item now?!"

"I don't know what happened. I chased after her and we turned around and you guys weren't there...and so, we just kind of hung out," Sam said sheepishly.

"And?" Brian continued.

"And yes, I know you like her too. But we were having a good time and she asked if I wanted to go with her–which surprised me–and I said 'Yes,'" Sam replied.

"Oh," Brian said, then stayed quiet for a bit as if he was working on an equation in his mind, then added something more or less to himself. "I guess that's for the best. It wouldn't have worked out, anyway. I don't live here throughout the year and that just wouldn't work. She's cute, though."

A minute later, they saw the familiar, two-tone brown truck pull into the parking area. The boys ran to the truck and it was just Uncle Bob behind the wheel. It was a regular-sized cab and there wouldn't have been enough room had Aunt Christie come along. As Chris opened the passenger door to let Sam and Brian hop in first, Uncle Bob said, "Get in boys. We didn't realize the storm was here until just a few minutes ago at the house. I came as quick as I could."

"It's okay, Dad. We were drenched already," Sam said.

"Yeah, it surprised all of us, I think," Chris added.

Uncle Bob put the truck into gear and headed for the exit. With everyone else leaving at the same time and only one exit, they got in line to wait behind other cars leaving. It was still warm out, but the storm caused the temperature to drop significantly. In the cab of the truck, the air conditioner was on full blast and for Chris, who literally had water dripping off his clothes, it was freezing.

"Did you boys have fun?" Uncle Bob asked.

"Yeah. It was a good time," Sam said.

Chris remained quiet but Brian spoke up, "It was all right, but...Sam has a girlfriend...Sam has a girlfriend." The last part he said annoyingly as his dug elbow into Sam's side, giving him a hard time.

"Shut up!" Sam said.

"Sam's got...Well, it's true," Brian said.

"Oh yeah? Who is it?" Uncle Bob asked.

"Erin," Sam said quietly and subdued, not wanting to bring any more attention to it than there already was.

"She's a nice girl." Uncle Bob looked at his son and winked as he smiled and said, "Good job."

Sam rolled his eyes, wishing he could disappear into his seat. Chris remained quiet and continued to look out the window. It was dark out, but the headlights of the other trucks and cars lit up the area. He looked out beyond the parking area and into the fields. It was really dark out that way and he could only see when lightning flashed. During one of the flashes, he thought he saw a figure or something, in the distance. When another flash lit up the area again, whatever it was, was gone. The rain made a steady and rapid tempo of beats on the roof of the truck, which sounded much like the white noise of a TV channel that had gone off the air for the night. As Chris listened, the volume increased. The noise changed subtly and slowly until Chris thought he heard words forming in the buzz of the noise. He focused more on the sound and the words became more audible in the drumming. It sounded as if it were saying "I know."

Chris recoiled quickly and looked at the other occupants of the truck, but no one else seemed to hear it. "I know that you know," the words continued. Chris had no idea if his mind was playing tricks on him, which led him to wonder, "Do crazy people know they are crazy?" He wasn't sure and he had no idea what the words he heard meant. "I'll be coming for you shortly." There it was again.

Whatever the words referred to immediately scared Chris and he replied to the void, "I don't know what you're talking about." Again, he looked to Brian, Sam, and Uncle Bob but they were lost in a conversation about something else. Funny, he hadn't noticed but he couldn't hear what they were saying. Their lips were moving but no sound made it to Chris' ears. Only the sound of white noise registered in Chris's mind, one that changed in volume and tempo as it seemingly spoke to Chris alone.

"Yes, you do."

The noise seemed that it was about to speak more but Chris felt an elbow in his side as he jolted awake. "Wake up, Chris. We're home now. Get out," his brother said as he elbowed his ribs. There wasn't much room in the truck seat, so it didn't take much movement to get Chris' attention. Chris looked around. Uncle Bob got out of the driver's side and Sam followed him out that side. Chris couldn't believe he had fallen asleep. He wasn't even tired.

He opened the door and let himself and Brian out of the truck. They followed the other two as they all ran inside, not that it helped, because they were already soaked. Chris went upstairs to change out of his wet clothes and sat there afterwards, thinking about the events of the night. "Yup," he thought to himself, "I should have stayed home in Florida this summer."

Chapter Thirteen

Sunday morning came early for the household. Chris had trouble sleeping throughout the night. The dream or whatever it was, scared him and his mind worked overtime to try and understand it. Most dreams disappeared or dissipated shortly after waking up, but not that one. It had staying power and it was one that Chris was pretty sure was going to stick around with him for the rest of his life. Once he did finally get to sleep, it was one of those restless types of sleep where you could never really tell if you were truly asleep or just had your eyes closed. It most definitely was not a restful night. They went through their Sunday morning rituals and headed to church. "At least Jessica will be there," thought Chris, going over last night's scene in his mind. "See you tomorrow," she had said.

They pulled into the parking lot of the small, white, wood-framed church and the bell was ringing, announcing to everyone that church service was about to begin. When Chris walked inside the foyer, he saw the pastor standing there, greeting folks as they arrived. The pastor's son, who was about eight, was using his whole body to pull the bell rope which dangled from the steeple overhead.

"Good morning, Mr. Williams. What did you do

to fix the bell?" Chris asked.

"Oh, it was the strangest thing. We were here yesterday, cleaning the church and sweeping the foyer and when we opened the door to sweep it all outside, there was this man walking down the street. He said he heard that our bell was broken. Well, knowing that it was a problem, I took him up on his offer to come in and take a look. After a couple of pulls on the rope, it started ringing like it was brand new," Mr. Williams said.

"Really?" Chris asked.

"Yeah! And he didn't even charge us for it," Mr. Williams said, "which was even more surprising because I think he's that hermit that lives just outside town. He's been living up there a few months, I believe. You'd think he would need the money for supplies or something."

With that, Mr. Williams greeted the next family coming through the front door, leaving Chris deep in thought. Chris stood to the side of the foyer and looked up at the ceiling where the rope disappeared through a hole just large enough for it to fit through. How could the hermit have fixed it by merely pulling on the rope? Chris was sure that Pastor Williams had already tried that. What made the difference when Ol' Ned did it? There was no way to get to the bell unless you used a ladder to access the steeple from the roof. It just didn't make sense.

Chris stayed in the foyer a moment longer and then continued into the sanctuary to take his usual seat with his family. He looked around and didn't see the

Darling family there this morning, which was unusual. Mr. Darling rarely came, if ever, but the mom and two daughters were almost always there. The empty pew where they usually sat looked odd and only magnified the feeling of disconnect, kind of like two plus two suddenly not equaling four, or something similar. It was a nagging feeling like when there's a small gnat that won't quit buzzing around your ear or a loose hair tickling your face.

Other than the Darling family not being there, the rest of the service was normal, even to the point of being mundane–same old songs, same old type of sermon. There was comfort, however, in the stability of being able to rely on some things that never seemed to change. Before too long, the service was over and Chris was outside with the sun shining brightly on his face. Even though it was warm, his face tingled with the breeze that with it, seemed to bring a good energy of its own. Little moments like these could teach a person about the joys of life, if they only kept an eye out for them; it wasn't lost on Chris and he took a moment to enjoy it. The moment didn't last very long because Sam walked over to him and said, "I wonder why Erin didn't come to church today."

"Yeah, I was wondering where they are, too. It was kinda strange looking over there and not seeing them there," Brian said.

Chris was glad that he wasn't the only one that noticed or felt the way he did about it. Aunt Christie and Uncle Bob followed them out of the church and got into truck, with the boys hopping into the bed, then drove home. When they got there, the boys piled out of the back and Chris turned toward Sam and his brother and asked, "Want to walk down to their house and see if they are okay?"

"Sure! That sounds great," Sam said.

"I guess so," Brian chimed in.

They all went inside and upstairs to change into clothes they didn't mind getting dirty, then headed back downstairs to the kitchen to grab a quick bite. With their stomachs full, they headed out, but not before letting Aunt Christie know where they were heading. The road in front of the house was at the top of a large, sweeping hill that didn't really feel like a hill due the long slope that went for miles in either direction. The view was a pretty one; you could almost see the patchwork of the different farms and pastures in the distance. The Darling house was maybe half a mile down the same road and it would only take a few minutes to get there. There were a few other farms and households, consisting of either farmhouses or single-wide trailers, that they passed on either side of the road. One of these homes had a dog that would always run up to the edge of the yard that bordered the road and bark at anyone passing by. Every time Chris tried to make friends, the dog would only bark and run away. "Stupid dog," Chris thought to himself. He liked animals and didn't understand why the dog never let him come closer. All the summers he'd come, that dog never got friendlier. "I guess sometimes," Chris thought, "it's good to keep people at arm's length." He thought of Ol' Ned. Maybe it wasn't a stupid dog after all.

They continued on and saw the Darling house in

the distance, after making the last turn. There were more cars in the driveway than usual, which wasn't particularly alarming, because the boys knew that the Darling family was a large one. In fact, the surname "Darling" was one that popped up all over southern Illinois, or so it seemed to Chris. As they got closer, they noticed there were a bunch of folks in the pasture and some walking throughout other areas of the farm. Their house was situated in a small dip between hills, so it wasn't hard to see the land beyond it. When they got close enough to be able to make out faces, they saw Jessica, Erin, their parents, and some other people in the pasture near the barn where they kept their horses. Chris immediately started to get a sinking feeling in the pit of his stomach. Something wasn't right. He could tell at a distance, by the looks on everyone's faces, they seemed concerned or confused about something. Whatever it was, he was sure they were about to find out.

They walked up and no one paid them any mind, so they went straight past the house, over to the fence that separated the pasture from the yard. Chris propped up and waved at Jessica, who eventually saw him and came over. Erin wasn't far behind.

"Hey. Everything okay? We didn't see you at church. What's going on?" Chris asked when she got within conversational range.

"Hey, guys," she replied. "It's our horse, Rocket. He's missing."

"Really?" Chris asked.

"Yeah, but the gate was closed and there aren't

any holes in the fence. All the other horses are still here."

"Wow. That's so strange," Chris said, as he looked over the fence and into the enclosed pasture. Like Jessica said, the whole area looked to be in order.

"And it's not like someone would steal him. He wasn't a spring chicken. I mean…if someone was going to steal a horse, there were better horses here," she said, as she gestured toward the other horses grazing in the field.

"When did you notice he was missing?" Chris asked.

"Well, Dad got up early this morning and let him out of his stall, then later as we were getting ready to go into town to church, we noticed that he was gone. So, we started searching and later called family to come help," Jessica said.

By this time, Erin had come over and was having her own conversation with Sam and Brian, a few feet away. Chris turned his attention back to Jessica, "How are you, though?"

She stopped to think about the question. "Me? I'm fine…just perplexed. We have no idea where Rocket could have gotten off to. Everyone is checking the rest of the farm and roads nearby but so far, no one has seen anything."

Chris' question was really referring more to how she felt about everything that happened the previous night. But, he didn't want to change the subject since she was obviously upset over her missing horse.

"Is there anything we can do?" Chris asked. "We'd love to help."

Brian, overhearing this, took a break from his conversation with Sam and Erin and piped in. "Yeah–what do you need?"

"I'm not sure. We've already searched everywhere. There really isn't anything else to do, that I know of. I think Dad is going to call the police or someone to keep a look out for Rocket. So...I'm not sure. We have never had this happen before. I mean...we have had horses get out after a storm, with a downed fence or something, but they didn't get very far. That wasn't the case this time unless he jumped the fence," she said, but then thought about it and added, "but I don't think that's what happened. He was getting older."

"Well, the mystery of why they weren't at church is solved, but only more mysteries seem to open up," thought Chris. There were so many questions he had this summer. He wasn't sure he'd find the answer to half of them...but such is life.

"Okay. Well, if you need anything..." Chris said, indicating that they were willing to help. He felt a little silly saying so, because there were already quite a few people here. He was pretty sure Sam, Brian and he wouldn't be the first people they'd call upon for help, but he wanted to offer, just the same.

There was an awkward lull in the conversation, as Jessica was deep in thought and confusion. Chris was also confused about what to do next. He quickly decided the conversation was over and there was nothing more to say or do. Jessica was preoccupied, as she should be. He'd feel the same way if something like that happened to him or his family. He wished he had more to add.

"Well, I guess we will go, then," he said, more just to say something rather than let the quiet linger any longer.

"Oh…right…yeah. I guess that's probably a good idea. I'm sorry," Jessica said. "I was really looking forward to going to church and hanging out this morning but then this happened, and my mind is all over the place now."

"It's okay. Don't worry about it," Chris said. "Maybe we can come over later this week and hang out or something."

"Sure. That sounds great," Jessica said, but Chris wasn't sure if she really meant it or was just being nice. It looked like the conversation between Erin and the other two was coming to an end, as well. They said their goodbyes and the boys waved one final time, with the girls returning the gesture.

"This has been one weird summer," Brian said, as they were halfway down the road and had reached the curve in the lane. They kept their eyes peeled as they walked. They'd stop every so often and peer in the fields alongside the road, looking for the missing horse. Deep down, however, Chris knew they wouldn't find Rocket. He didn't know how or why he knew this, but he knew.

"Agreed," Chris said, responding to his brother's

statement. "We probably don't even know the half of it," he thought to himself.

"Want to go fishing?" Sam asked.

Chris just looked at Sam. "What? How could you be thinking of going fishing right now?"

Sam was caught off-guard and maybe a little embarrassed. "Oh…I don't know. I didn't mean today, necessarily. Maybe tomorrow. I was just thinking of things to do."

"No. I don't really want to go fishing," Chris said. "Not with that hermit hanging around. I don't want to run into him."

"Why not? He seems like a nice guy," Sam said.

"I don't know–just something about him. Besides, tomorrow I want to go into town and check on Mrs. Willing at the store," Chris said.

"Who?" Sam asked.

Chapter Fourteen

Chris and Brian came to an abrupt stop in the middle of the road and looked at Sam as if he were growing a second head. "Mrs. Willing, the lady at the country store in town?" Chris responded.

"I don't know who that is," Sam said.

"Quit playing around," Brian said.

"What are you talking about?" Sam asked. He looked genuinely confused, matching the expressions of the other two boys.

"You seriously expect us to believe that you don't remember her?" Chris asked.

"Yeah…as a matter of fact, I do," Sam said, completely serious. "The only lady I know at the store is Mrs. Hannover…and so do you. Why are you guys acting so weird?"

At the mention of Mrs. Hannover, memories of a lady with that name bloomed inside Chris' mind. Mrs. Willing was a short, roundish lady with shoulder-length, brown, curly hair, whereas this new lady (or rather, the memories of her) was tall and slender, with long, straight, black hair and who never wore makeup. It was like a rushing of wind, but in this case, memories–memories that coincided with the same memories he had of Mrs. Willing in some instances.

157

It left Chris speechless for a few moments. He could only assume that Brian was experiencing something similar, by the look on his face. Sam remained in front of them, watching them both.

"Stop it, guys. You're scaring me," Sam finally said.

Chris and Brian looked at each other but couldn't put into words what they were thinking. They, or at least Chris, had to have some time to reflect and process what was going on.

"Are you sure you don't remember a lady named Mrs. Willing?" Chris asked.

"No, I don't," Sam said, as he raised his right hand into a scout's salute. "Scout's honor! I swear."

"You were never a boy scout," Brian said.

"So...I still mean it," Sam replied.

"Let's get back to the house," Chris said, and started walking. The other two boys momentarily stood there but eventually started walking toward home. Chris wanted to go ask Aunt Christie about Mrs. Willing. Surely, she would remember her and if she didn't, then he didn't know what to do. It was all just so strange and hard for Chris to wrap his mind around. So far, there had been quite a few odd things happen this summer, but this was outright crazy. It was like grasping at water, which you never really could do. You stick your hand in water and start grabbing and only end up with a wet hand. As Chris got closer to the house, he picked up the pace; when they arrived, he wasted no time going inside.

Aunt Christie was sitting at the kitchen table and saw him come in. "So, how were they?" she asked, wanting to know how the Darling family was doing.

"They couldn't find one of their horses this morning, after letting him out to graze. They can't find him anywhere," Chris replied.

Brian and Sam came in after him and went over to the couch to sit and listen in on the conversation. Aunt Christie was snapping green beans and throwing them into a pot, so Chris sat down and started to help. The pantry was full of canned goods that Aunt Christie canned herself. Many of the vegetables had even been grown in their large garden. It was quite the process and something that Chris had always found fascinating– both gardening and canning the harvests.

"Aunt Christie?" he asked.

"Yes?" she replied, snapping more green beans.

"Do you remember Mrs. Willing from the country store down in Stonemill?" Chris asked.

She momentarily stopped snapping the bean she currently had in hand and looked up at the ceiling, pensively. "Willing...hmm..." She murmured, deep in thought, "You know, that name does sound familiar but I'm not placing it. You said she worked at the store?"

"Yes. You know–the lady behind the counter that usually cuts the ham in the deli, then wraps it up for you? She's short and kinda stout, with dark, curly hair. You know who I'm talking about...right?"

"Are you sure you're not getting her confused

with Mrs. Hannover?" she asked.

Now Chris knew, or at least was pretty sure, that he wasn't crazy, but this about put him over the edge. He dropped the subject and backed away from it. He had to have some time to think.

"No. It's okay. I was just curious," Chris said.

"Yeah...like I said, sounds vaguely familiar but no, I don't think I do," she said as she went back to snapping the beans. Chris remained quiet while Sam and Aunt Christie talked...about what, Chris didn't know because he was lost in thought. He was going through the motions–snap, snap, throw, snap, snap, throw. The monotony of snapping the beans seemed a nice respite compared to the waves of turmoil in Chris' thoughts.

Before long, it was time to go back to church for Sunday evening service, which came and went pretty quickly. The Darling family were a no show again, to which Chris wasn't surprised. There was a lot of activity over at their house earlier in the day. Chris wanted to ask others in the congregation about Mrs. Willing but decided not to. He didn't need any more evidence of him possibly losing his mind. The only thing that kept him sane was the fact that his brother was going through the same experience that he was. It was funny, Chris thought...well, maybe not funny...but it always seems better to go through something difficult with someone else. "What's the saying? 'Misery loves company,'" he thought to himself. They hadn't had a chance to talk about it at length yet, because they were always around other people. He made a mental note to hash this out with

Brian either later tonight or sometime tomorrow. It was too strange to ignore and pretend like nothing was going on.

When they got home after church, Chris realized the day's events had worn him out. Too many thoughts, too many emotions and honestly, he hadn't had time to truly bounce back from the excitement at the carnival the night before. Today's unexplained events just rubbed salt into the wound, so to speak.

Chris went straight upstairs to the bedroom and even though it was only around 8:30, he crawled in bed and went right to sleep. It was a fitful sleep and around midnight, he woke up. It was hot in the room and if it wasn't for the small box fan with its constant hum, it would have been miserable. As it was, it was moving hot air but at least the air wasn't stagnant. He laid there for a while, trying to get back to sleep. It was pitch black in the room. In the country, when the lights are off and there is either a new moon or the moonlight is obscured by shadows, it can get inky black in some areas. It's even worse inside, despite open windows.

Chris decided to get up. He could hear his brother snoring softly and his cousin's steady, rhythmic breathing. Since it was so dark and he couldn't see, he went off memory and moved slowly, so he wouldn't stub his toe on anything. He could have turned on the lamp near his bed, but he didn't want to wake the other two up. When he found the door frame with his outstretched hand and made it to the landing at the top of the stairs, he breathed a sigh of relief, grabbed onto the banister and headed downstairs. He could see a little bit of light spilling into the front room, from the kitchen. "Good," he thought, "I'm not the only one up." When Chris walked into the kitchen, he saw his uncle sitting in his recliner in the living room, which was adjacent to the kitchen. He had a large glass of milk in his hand. Chris decided it had to be one of two things: 1) a large glass of buttermilk (which Chris had never acquired a taste for and in fact, found it rather disgusting), or 2) saltine crackers crunched up in regular milk and eaten like breakfast cereal. When he saw the spoon sticking out of the glass, he knew it was the latter.

"Can't sleep?" Uncle Bob asked.

"No, sir," Chris replied. "You?"

"No. Not at all."

"Is that going to help?" Chris indicating the milk with crackers.

"Probably not," Uncle Bob replied.

Chris went in and sat on the couch that was against the far wall. The TV, which only had three channels, at best (and totally depending on how well the antenna was tuned), was turned off. It was a quiet moment in the country household.

"How are things going this summer, Chris?" asked Uncle Bob, breaking the silence.

"It's been strange. By the way, do you know much about that hermit?" Chris asked. He wasn't sure why the hermit popped up in his mind but that was the only major difference between this summer and all the other previous summers.

"No, not really. No one really knows much, but then again, I don't really keep up with others. I just know he's been here a couple months...maybe a few. Why do you ask?"

"I don't know...there's just something "off" about him," Chris said.

"Yeah, I think I know what you mean. He's always been friendly, from what I've seen, but I'd stay away from him."

"Why'd you give him permission to fish at the pond?" Chris asked.

"Oh...I don't know. Seemed like he would have been able to anyway. It's not like I can be out there all the time to keep anyone out. Heck, I have trouble with hunters coming on the land from time to time and at least he asked, so it wasn't a big deal," Uncle Bob replied.

"Yeah. Makes sense," Chris said.

Chris was going to ask if Uncle Bob remembered the lady down at the store but was interrupted when his uncle got up and said that he was going to make another attempt at going to sleep.

"Make sure you turn off the light when you go to bed, now," Uncle Bob said.

"I will," Chris said.

With that, Uncle Bob said goodnight and headed upstairs. Chris could hear the creaking of the wood stairs as his uncle climbed them. Then it was quiet again and Chris was alone with his thoughts. Before long, Chris' eyes started to feel heavy again and he decided that he should try and make another attempt at sleeping, as well. He turned off the kitchen light and returned the way he came.

The next morning, Chris woke up with a start. Brian stood over him and Chris realized that his brother was shaking his shoulder.

"What are you doing?" he asked grumpily.

"You were making noises and they didn't sound good...like you were having a bad dream," Brian said.

"Oh," Chris said. He didn't remember having a dream. The only thing he remembered was coming back upstairs last night and going right to sleep, thankfully. He did feel pretty groggy and "out of it" now, though. In fact, he thought he could probably roll over and go back to sleep for another couple of hours.

"Come on. Get up," Brian said.

"Leave me alone. I want to go back to sleep," Chris said.

"Chris—we need to get up and go into town. I want to find out what happened to Mrs. Willing," Brian said.

At the mere mention of Mrs. Willing, Chris came instantly awake. He, too, wanted to find out what happened.

"Okay. Sounds good. Let me get ready real quick."

Chris looked at the time; it was almost 8:00. He

got out of bed. He felt a little disgusting due to sweating through the night, so took a quick shower before he started the day. After getting dressed and brushing his teeth, he headed downstairs. Brian and Sam were already ready to go. They must have gotten up super early, then Chris thought, "Maybe I didn't have a dream, after all. Maybe Brian just used that as an excuse to wake me up." It wouldn't have surprised him. His brother could be sneaky like that, but then again, he could too. They said goodbye to Aunt Christie, let her know where they were going and when they expected to return, then left through the door by the kitchen. It was overcast outside–the kind of day that could immediately dump rain or miraculously clear to blue skies, depending on things Chris had no knowledge of.

They walked down the gravel road and after going around a couple of bends, the gravel ended at the hardtop that went into town. Chris had walked this way so many times that it was almost like being on autopilot. He thought it was funny how far this route had seemed when he was younger. In years previous, he thought it took half a day to get to the end of the lane but as he grew older…well, now he realized it only took at most, ten minutes.

As they continued on the hardtop, the fishing pond would be coming up on the right. Chris hoped that they wouldn't see the hermit but as luck would have it, there he was, standing on the side of the road as if he were waiting for them.

Chapter Fifteen

"Hello, boys. Come to go fishing?" he asked.

"Hey, Ol' Ned," Sam said, "I..."

"No. We were just heading into town," Chris said, cutting Sam off before he had a chance to finish what he was about to say.

"Are you sure? I have some extra fishing poles. Surely, it couldn't hurt to pass a little time," Ol' Ned said. He smiled, but ever since Chris noticed how his smile never reached his eyes, that was the only thing he saw now. The smile was just a façade and didn't reflect the true face behind it.

"I sure would love to, but they want to head into town," Sam said.

"What's in town that has you so focused on getting there?" Ol' Ned asked.

"Oh, nothing really. They just want to go ch..." Sam said, but again was interrupted by Chris. "Nothing in particular. We just wanted to go check and see if the store has restocked the Mello Yello. They haven't had it the past couple of times we've stopped in," Chris answered.

This, of course, was a lie, but Chris couldn't come up with anything better on the spur of the moment.

Why was Sam being so open with the hermit?

"Suit yourself," the hermit said. "But before you go, do you boys have anything you need help with?"

Ol' Ned's eyes twinkled with intensity as he asked the question, causing further disconnect between his smile and his eyes.

"No, but thanks," Chris and Brian said, almost simultaneously.

"Are you sure, Chris? Perhaps I can help with your relationship with that girl Jessica, just like I helped young Sam here with Erin."

This comment slapped Chris across the face, kind of like opening the front door on an extremely hot day and meeting a wave of hot air unexpectedly–the kind of heat that caused a recoil of horror. Before Chris could even begin to think of something coherent to say, the hermit turned his attention to Brian.

"Or I could help you with..." He took a moment to peer at Brian, as if looking straight into his soul. "Ah...yes...I could help you with seeing your dad sooner than you thought."

The more the hermit spoke, the more alarming it became. Sam was the only one that seemed okay with everything but for Chris and Brian, the encounter only made them dig their heals into the absurdity of what they were hearing.

"Come on...you can trust me. I've already shown you how to fish better, shared delicious food with you. I can help you in other ways," the hermit said, trying to make everything sound enticing. Had Chris not been thinking of Mrs. Willing, he very well may have been enticed. The hermit had indeed seemed nice, but something definitely seemed awry, ever since that morning in the store when Mrs. Willing forgot the hermit had been there just minutes before. That incident, along with the fact that everyone tasted something completely different and seemed to experience some sort of time lapse the day they went to his cabin...it all made Chris extremely suspicious.

"No, thanks," Chris said.

Apparently, Brian had the same idea, because he said stiffly, "No. I don't want anything from you."

Chris looked at Brian, but Brian's attention was on Sam. He noticed Brian looked a little crestfallen; he was looking at Sam as though he was seeing something new and wasn't sure what he thought about it. Chris could only imagine, but he thought it might have been something to do with Erin.

The hermit saw their reactions and switched gears, saying nonchalantly, "Oh that's fine. No worries. I will help you out with something eventually. It's what I like to do."

"We have to get going," Chris said, and continued walking with the other boys following.

"Have a great day and be safe," the hermit said and cheerily added, "There's a lot of bad things out there."

The whole encounter unnerved Chris. He didn't speak until they were far away–in fact, he didn't speak or slow down from his forced march until after they passed the Bliss-Deaton cemetery. Once they reached that point, Chris stopped and turned on Sam. "What did you do!?"

"What do you mean?" Sam asked.

"What did he do for you?" Chris demanded.

"Oh...well...at the carnival, I saw him and he said 'Hello,'" Sam replied.

"Go on," Chris said.

"Well, he saw me with Erin and when Erin turned away to look at something, Ol' Ned looked at me and kinda whispered that he could help get Erin to like me. I said 'sure,'" Sam answered. "I didn't really think he'd be able to do anything, but then something happened."

"What did he do to help you?"

"I don't know, but it seemed almost immediate that Erin asked me to go with her."

Chris could see that this distressed Brian. Heck– he would have been mad, too. "Why didn't you tell us that?"

"You didn't ask!" Sam said, his voice rising in defense because he was put on the spot.

"Yes, we did. You just didn't include that part," Brian finally said, quietly.

"What's the big deal?" Sam questioned. "You guys are acting like I did something horrible. So what? I forgot to mention that part."

"Sam, I don't know what you did but something

isn't right about that guy. Don't you feel it, too?" Chris asked.

"Well...yeah...I guess...sort of. But he helped me out and now Erin likes me, so who cares?" Sam replied.

"We care," Brian said.

"Whatever," Sam said, getting irritated at the conversation. "Let's just drop it."

Chris was alarmed. He could feel it deep in his gut, in full force. Something indeed wasn't right about all of this. Who is this hermit and why does he seem to be helping people for no apparent reason? He was reminded of something his mom once said– "Look out for deals, son. There's almost always a catch to them. If something seems too good to be true, it usually is."

As they continued the rest of the way into town, the mood was quiet and the tension between the boys was palpable. Chris' mom's advice kept rolling through his head as they walked through the quiet village of Stonemill. There wasn't much movement this Monday morning, but they did see one or two people sitting on their front porch having a cup of coffee. One nice thing about small towns like this one is that people usually wave at one another and they don't necessarily have to know them. The sun was rising, as well as the heat, when they finally made it to the small store. They opened the door and a refreshing coolness overcame them, as the air conditioner was on and greeted them like an old friend.

Chris had wanted to get here as soon as possible to find out what happened to Mrs. Willing, but she was nowhere to be seen. Her usual place behind the counter was taken by a tall lady with dark hair named Mrs. Hannover. The strange thing about it was that Chris now had memories of her rolling around in his head, along with memories of Mrs. Willing. The memories of Mrs. Willing, though, didn't seem as strong, as if they were fading.

"Mrs.?" Chris asked to the lady to get her attention.

"Chris, you know me. What do you need?" she replied.

And indeed, he did know her. The more she spoke, the stronger his memories of her materialized. All of a sudden, it felt very strange to ask about Mrs. Willing, like she was a figment of his imagination, but he had to ask because even though his memories of her were fading, some still lingered in his mind.

"Do you know a Mrs. Willing?" Chris asked.

"Hmm...no. Doesn't ring a bell," Mrs. Hannover replied.

"How long have you worked here?" Chris continued.

Mrs. Hannover gave Chris a quizzical look and smiled. "Well, a number of years– long enough to know you and your whole family, like Sam here and his parents. Long enough to know that you and your brother come here every summer. Why do you ask?"

She had a pleasantness to her and there was really nothing alarming about her...except that years of memories seemed to magically appear in Chris' mind.

It was something that he just couldn't comprehend. It was as if Mrs. Willing never existed; life would continue on and no one would remember her or have memories of the years she spent behind this counter. She had lived here, and she worked here until this past weekend...didn't she? Chris was so confused, and the memories of Mrs. Willing were already becoming stale.

"See, I told you she was the lady that worked here," Sam said.

And Chris knew he was correct, at least on some level, that Mrs. Hannover was the lady that worked here, at least in these new memories or on this new timeline. He wasn't sure which it was or what exactly happened, but something happened this past weekend that dramatically changed the course of things. The only explanation he could think of was the hermit. He was always around when things got weird. Chris still remembered all the "out of place" things from his cabin and the unexplained events that seemed to have occurred every time he was around, or had been around. He did something–Chris wasn't yet sure what that was, but it had to be him. He was the last one seen with Mrs. Willing.

Immediately, proverbial alarms went off in his mind. "We need to go check on Jessica and Erin," Chris said.

"What? Why?" Sam asked. "We just got here."

Even Brian looked at Chris questioningly.

"Maybe it's nothing but I want to go check on something," Chris said, not adding much to his request because he didn't want to voice something and regret it later.

Since they were at the store, they decided to go ahead and grab a couple of soft drinks. The big drink companies had come out with the twenty-ounce, resealable, plastic bottles the year before, which was a big step up from the sixteen-ounce bottles and the twelve-ounce cans. It was still a novelty...but then again, Chris didn't remember the store having these the last time they came in, when Mrs. Willing was still working behind the counter. Noticing that the store now carried these bottles, Chris looked around at other things in the store. Some items weren't where they used to be, and some of the shelves and aisles were placed differently. It was so strange to have two memories competing with each other for dominance.

"Are you ok?" Mrs. Hannover asked him. "You look pale. Are you sick?

"Oh...no, Mrs. Hannover, I am...I just have a lot on my mind," he replied.

They paid for their drinks and left the store; it was still early morning, but the humidity was heavy today. That, coupled with the heat, brought on a mugginess that could only be helped with a strong breeze, which was in short supply this morning.

Brian quietly asked Chris before Sam walked out of the store to join them, "Did you notice the changes in the store?"

Chris nodded. "I did."

Knowing his brother saw them, too, made Chris

feel a little better. It was still weird but knowing he wasn't crazy or alone made it more bearable.

"What do you think is going on?" Brian asked.

"I don't know," Chris replied.

Sam came out of the store and caught up with them, "What are y'all talking about?" he asked.

"Oh, nothing," Brian said, and Chris understood the deflection. Sam wasn't experiencing any of these strange observations like they were.

Chris was about to make a "your mama" joke like he would have with his friends back home, in order to change the subject, but realized he would be talking about Aunt Christie…and that just didn't seem so funny. Whatever was going on here in the small town of Stonemill, it didn't seem to affect the people who lived here full-time. The regular residents continued on like nothing happened but not for Chris and Brian. What was the difference? Was it that they didn't live here? He wasn't sure. All these questions and more wouldn't stop tumbling around in his head.

"Hey…let's stop by the church and see if Pastor Williams is there," Sam said.

From where they were, which was the main road through Stonemill, the church was just a couple blocks down on the other side of the street. They could actually see the church from the front of the store, but the parking lot of the church was empty.

"I don't think he's there," Chris said.

"Yeah, probably not," Sam said. "I was just

thinking of something to do since we were here already."

"Well, we can still walk by there on the way back. I mean…it's not like it's out of our way," Chris said.

"'We could go see what's happening at the park. The carnival is still in town," Sam said.

Chris had almost forgotten about the carnival, even though his thoughts were on Mrs. Willing and the last place he saw her. It seemed like it had been years since they had gone, instead of only a day and half.

"Sure…why not?" Chris said and they walked down the road toward the park. The carnival was still there, but not for long. The rides were being dismantled and packed for transport to the next destination. The bustling reminded Chris of an ant hill that had been disturbed and ants crawling all over the place in response.

"They weren't here very long," Brian said.

"Huh…no they weren't," Chris agreed.

"Well, it is Stonemill," Sam said. "If you blink, you'd miss it and honestly, I'm surprised they even came at all…and doubly surprised at the number of people that showed up."

The conversation died as the boys looked on. They stood just outside the park, watching, until Sam piped up with a suggestion. "Since we don't really have anything else to do, why don't we get closer and see what's going on? I've never seen a traveling carnival pack up before."

Chris was mildly interested and thought that it would be something interesting to see, as well as possibly get his mind off things for a while. Brian only shrugged his acceptance to the idea and the boys walked closer to get a better look. On the way, Chris was reminded of the strange lady, Madame Zara, and a thought crossed his mind—maybe she might have an understanding of what's going on here in Stonemill. Couldn't hurt to ask, he thought. He was desperate for answers and grasping at straws.

He turned toward his brother and Sam, telling them that he wanted to go check on something and that he'd be back shortly.

"What? Where you going?" Sam asked.

"I'm going to go clarify something with the carnival psychic," Chris replied.

Brian had a look of confusion, the same look that Sam had, but when Chris explained where he was heading, Brian's expression changed to speculative curiosity. He knew why Chris was going to see the old lady, even if Sam didn't. Immediately to shift attention away from Chris, Brian excitedly said, "Hey let's go look at them dismantle the Scrambler. I've always been interested to see how they do that."

Brian ran on, not waiting for Sam. Sam looked toward Brian as he ran off, then back at Chris, who had already headed toward where they had met Madame Zara. He had to make a decision. He just shrugged and ran after Brian, because he was also curious about how they dismantled some of the rides.

"Swift thinking, Brian," Chris thought to himself.

"That little brother of mine can sure surprise me at times." He ventured forth into the center of the carnival. It looked completely different than it had the night before last. He probably wasn't supposed to be there, but no one bothered him. They were busy with their own tasks of getting packed up and on down the road. It didn't take him long to get to Madame Zara's location. The tent was no longer there. Instead, there was a small motorhome with a pull-behind, enclosed trailer attached. And there she was, at the back of the trailer with a couple of other carnies, pushing, pulling and shoving the remnants of the tent into the trailer. He almost didn't recognize her as she didn't have all of her stage makeup on. She looked old–even more so than she did the other night–and tired. "Must be a rough life," Chris thought, "being constantly on the go, town after town…but it's probably a little exciting too–getting to see all kinds of new places."

He walked up to the trailer and tried to get her attention. "Madame Zara?"

Chapter Sixteen

She stopped and stiffened, without even turning to look. "I knew it. I just knew it. Of course, you wouldn't leave me alone."

She then turned around and looked at Chris. "Listen kid, I don't want to be involved. Oh…and by the way, my name isn't Madame Zara; it's Kathy. Don't you know what an act is?"

She was gaining momentum as she spoke and continued to speak, but more or less only to herself at this point. "As if I needed any more problems this morning. I swear to God…I just want to get out of here and on to the next town."

The old lady then stopped and looked at Chris and not just an acknowledging glance. She really looked at him and then sighed, resignedly, saying "What do you want?"

For a moment, Chris was so surprised at the sudden shift that it took a few seconds for words to form.

"I…uh…listen…I know you saw something the other night. Whatever you saw, I'd just like to know a little bit more. You're leaving but I'm stuck here, and I just want a little more information. I don't know what's going on here."

The gushing of words from Chris' mouth caused the older woman to stop. "Well, at least you don't beat around the bush," she replied. She looked around at the activity around her, then back at Chris. "I guess I am leaving...and sometimes I forget what it's like being a kid and not having choices."

Chris would have normally been irritated by being equated to a kid, but at this point, he was on the verge of desperation for answers, so he let it slide. Madame Zara, or rather, "Kathy" (if that was indeed her name), stood tall as if facing something bravely, and gave Chris her undivided attention. "I'll talk to you, but you must leave immediately when I'm done."

"Yes, ma'am," Chris said.

"Good. Thank you," she replied and continued being completely real with him. "Listen, I only have a little bit of the gift. I only get flashes and feelings about things and I don't always know what they mean. I don't see things as clearly as some of the others I have known. You should have met the real Madame Zara, the one I took my name from. She was...she could tell what was going on in people's lives from a distance, even to the point of being able to tell what they had for breakfast that morning. You could never get one in on her...she just knew things. Not many people out there like her...and she's been gone for quite a while." She stopped, then continued, "I'm sorry. I get sidetracked easily."

"It's okay..." Chris was in the middle of saying but the old lady continued, without missing a beat.

"Well...anyway...about you and what I saw...or

felt. I got a feeling...or vision...or something...of threads being burned and about a general darkness. You understand, kid? Something dark and powerful is at play here. Anyway, the other night, I wasn't expecting that and you scared me. I'm telling you this because you should be scared, too."

Chris was scared, and all this conversation did was beg more questions–questions to which he was afraid he wouldn't find answers, or would find them too late to do any good. He suddenly became acutely aware of those in this town whom he cared about. If Mrs. Willing could suddenly disappear and no one remember her, what could become of his family–Sam, Aunt Christie, and Uncle Bob? What about the Darling sisters? Even Brian? What if they disappeared and no one remembered them? So many new questions, and no answers to try and find a solution.

"And that's all I got. I wish I had more, for your sake, but I don't. You seem like a nice kid. I'm happy to be leaving this town and if you can find a way to leave, you should, too," the old lady finished.

"Some of us don't have the luxury of choices," Chris thought. He obviously wanted to ask more questions, but he knew this well was dry and that the lady didn't have anything else to offer. Her tone and demeanor said it all: she was finished.

"Okay...well...thank you. I still don't understand, really, but I appreciate you explaining it a little," Chris said.

"Well, I wish you luck," she said, then turned back to the progress of getting out of Stonemill, leaving Chris alone with his thoughts, which were already in overdrive. He turned around and left the way he came. Before long, he reconnected with Brian and Sam, who were waiting for him.

"That sucked," Sam said.

"What happened?" Chris asked.

"They wouldn't even let us get close enough to watch them dismantle the ride," Sam said. "Then they just sort of glared at us until we left."

"I guess it's just secrets of the trade," Chris said, half-jokingly.

"No, I don't think that's it," Sam said, not catching on to the joke.

Brian just rolled his eyes and said, "Come on. Let's get out of here. It's miserable just standing here in the sun and heat."

When Brian mentioned the heat, the other two became more aware and agreed, anywhere would be better to discuss things instead of this wide-open area where there wasn't any shade to be seen. They decided to walk back to the house. The road had large trees with ample shade and that always seemed to lower the temperature a little. From their current location, the road out was on the other side of the village, so they headed that way. They passed by the church and headed up the side street beside it, which took them by Mrs. Duren's house. She sat on the front porch and waved at the boys as they walked past. They returned the wave and continued on. Chris had never really given it much thought, but the small village of Stonemill was the quintessential picture of country living, complete with a community that knew one another and took care of one another. It was the kind of place where people waved at friends and strangers, which made it all the more peculiar that no one seemed to realize that a lady was missing.

They passed the Catholic church and Father Bishop was out front. He walked over to greet them when he saw the boys coming up the street. Seeing him coming, they slowed down and stopped.

"Did you boys enjoy the carnival?" he asked.

"Yeah, it was a great time," Sam said and then continued, "Thanks for the job! We had plenty of money to do everything we wanted."

Father Bishop looked at Sam as if remembering something and then said, "Oh, yeah...no problem. I'm glad you boys enjoyed it." He then looked at Chris and Brian. "You boys are quiet; did you enjoy it equally, as well?"

"Yeah. It was okay," Chris said half-heartedly, which his brother echoed. Chris did have a good time, at least until he saw...wait...who was it? Mrs. Willing! His memories of her were fading, like a piece of paper that caught fire and crumbled, before turning to ash to be blown away by the wind. He had to actively think about her now to remember. Yes, it was Mrs. Willing and the hermit. He had a good time until he saw them together, but not so much after. That, combined with the information Madame Zara smacked him with, made it seem as if the world had gone awry since the evening of the carnival. Things were definitely crazy.

The priest looked at him with a discerning eye. "Would you like to talk about it?"

Coming out of his concentration, Chris looked back at Father Bishop. "Oh, no. Everything is fine; it was just a weird evening."

But the look on the father's face showed that he didn't quite believe Chris when he said everything was fine.

"Okay then, but Chris–or any of you boys– really…if you need to talk, I'm always available to chat...about anything." He looked at each of them individually, then continued on, "Strange storm that popped up that night–don't you think? I don't think I've ever seen one with as much lightning as that one had. Amazing no one was struck."

Before any of the boys could respond, he glanced down at his watch. "Oh, look at the time. I've got to go get things ready for mass. You boys be safe." Father Bishop then left the boys as he headed back inside the church.

The boys continued and when they weren't far outside of town, Sam, making conversation, asked, "Did you find that psychic lady?"

"Yes, I did, but it wasn't much help," Chris replied.

Brian's expression changed from a look of hope to one of frustration when he heard that Chris hadn't found out anything. He, too, was wrestling with questions, probably the same ones that were going through Chris' mind.

"That's too bad," Sam said.

"What did she say?" Brian asked.

At first, Chris was hesitant to say anything. He was fairly sure that the only people he knew that felt anything was "off" were Brian and him. He didn't want to go talking about it in front of Sam, who would just look at them both weird. But Chris relented, thinking that in the grand scheme of things, it didn't really matter and they might as well talk about it. Maybe Sam would come around in his way of thinking.

"She said that she saw or felt threads being burned and something really dark in my future," Chris said.

Sam stopped momentarily in the middle of the road. "Geeze, if that doesn't give you the heebie-jeebies, I don't know what will. Did she say anything else?"

"No."

"That's so weird," Sam said.

"Yeah…I don't exactly know what it all meant. I don't think she did either, though, to be honest," Chris said.

They continued on and thankfully, Chris thought, they didn't see the hermit on their way home. When they arrived at the house, Aunt Christie was preparing lunch and asked how their trip was. Sam went straight into telling her about the carnival and how it was packing up. Any news was new news for the small village, and Sam was happy to share it. By this time, it was just before noon, so they all sat around the kitchen table to eat lunch together. Only Uncle Bob was missing, as he was at work. It was a light lunch of ham and cheese sandwiches with sliced apples and carrots on the side. There was nothing fancy about it but it tasted great to Chris. He must have been a lot hungrier than he thought he was. As the conversation went around the table, Chris got caught up with his own thoughts. The summers seemed to last forever here and this summer, it was still early and going home to Florida was still quite a few weeks out. His mind was stuck in a loop of the events that had occurred so far but had come to no conclusion. What was it about that hermit? Of course, this was the primary question that continued to pop up in his mind over and over again.

"Chris?" Aunt Christie said. Apparently, she had called his name more than once.

He came out of his thoughts immediately when he realized she was talking to him, "Yes, ma'am?"

"Are you okay?"

"Yes. Just tired, I guess."

"Okay. Thought we lost you there for a second. Would you please pass the salt?" she asked.

"Oh, sure...sorry...guess I was for a second," Chris said, as he gave her the salt, which she proceeded to sprinkle on her apple slices.

After lunch, the boys helped clean up and with their afternoon wide open, they decided to head down to the Darling farm. It was still warm out, but the breeze had picked up, which made it a little more bearable. That's another plus of living near the top of the sweeping hill–more opportunity for breeze. They left the house and started along the gravel lane, seeing the same sights they saw yesterday. That little dog came running up to the edge of the yard again and, as usual, ran away when the boys tried to give it attention. They turned the corner and saw the Darling house come into view. There wasn't near the activity they saw yesterday; in fact, it was the complete opposite. Where there were a lot of cars and trucks there yesterday, the yard was nearly empty today. There was only the blue sedan that they used for family outings. Mr. Darling's truck wasn't there so they assumed he wasn't home. They continued down the final stretch and hopped up onto the front porch. As Chris opened the screen door to knock, the front door swung open and Erin and Jessica both appeared. The sudden movement caused Chris to jump back, accidentally letting go of the screen door, which then closed in the girls' faces.

Chris laughed at himself when he saw what he had done and said, "Oh, sorry! You scared me. I didn't expect you."

The girls reopened the screen door and grinned at Chris as they came out on the porch to join the boys. Chris' face had reddened slightly at the embarrassment of causing the screen door to shut on them. "Totally not smooth," he thought to himself. What they must think of him…he didn't really want to know. This was a lie, however. He really did want to know what they thought of him, just like most boys do when it comes to the opposite sex, especially those you sort of liked. The saving grace here was that the moment came and went so quickly that the small incident was pretty much forgotten before the conversation even began.

"Our mom saw you walking down the road, from the kitchen window, and let us know," Jessica said, giggling.

"Oh, that makes sense," Chris thought. What was funny was that he had lost count of the number of times he'd walked down that road, hoping the girls would see him and come out. The one time that they did, he shut the screen door in their faces. So much for irony and timing.

"What are y'all up to today?" Erin asked.

"We were coming to see if you found your horse, Rocket," Chris said, replying to Erin but looking over at Jessica. The girls heard the words and blinked at the boys. A look of confusion, then suspicion, came over their faces as Jessica responded, "What are you talking about?"

Chapter Seventeen

Chris immediately felt small flashes of electricity spark and snap all over his body in response to Jessica's question. "Oh, no," he thought, "Not this again." This sense of "offness" was becoming a common occurrence and Chris didn't like it. He was taken aback and looked at his brother, who also seemed surprised at the question. Chris then looked at Sam, who had the same expression that the girls had, like he had no clue what Chris was talking about. Brian interjected with his own question, "Your horse, Rocket–he went missing yesterday. In fact, we were here yesterday, and you had a whole boatload of people helping to look for him. You don't remember us coming over and talking about that?"

The girls' faces grew even more confused, or maybe apprehensive, like they didn't know if they were dealing with a crazy person or not. Sam looked at Chris and Brian like they were playing a joke and was upset that he wasn't in on it.

"Uh...no...we've never had a horse named "Rocket." You came to our house yesterday?" Erin asked.

"Uh...yeah," Chris said, but now wasn't so sure. The same sense of competing memories that he had between Mrs. Hannover and Mrs....Mrs...

189

um…Willing (!), was happening again. This time, he had one set of memories of coming here yesterday to check on them due to their absence at church, yet another set of memories of seeing them in church. He had a vague "recollection" of Erin and Sam sitting together during the service and also of a long conversation (and a good one, at that), he had with Jessica.

Chris felt on the brink of vertigo as his mind wrapped around these new memories. He looked past the girls at a spot on the wall behind them, in order to keep his bearing and balance, as well as his cool. He didn't want to become panicked in front of them. Maybe he was losing his mind. No…his little brother was also experiencing the same thing, so that wasn't the case, unless they were both losing their minds.

"Are you guys playing a joke on us?" Jessica asked.

"What? Oh, no...no...we weren't. Sorry. I guess I was confused about something," Chris said, trying to salvage the moment.

Chris looked at Brian. He knew that Chris wasn't confused.

"Oh-kay, then," Sam said, with an inflection of silliness to further prove that he wasn't in on the joke. It only added to the awkwardness of the situation.

"I don't know what he's going on about, but we decided to come see what y'all were up to," Sam continued. Although the comment was directed at everyone, he was looking at Erin when he spoke, as it was really just for her.

"We don't have anything planned today–just kind of hanging out, I guess," Erin said.

Jessica followed up, "It's kind of warm out here. Do you want to go inside and have some tea?"

Sam immediately said "Yes," while Brian and Chris nodded in agreement because they were wrestling with the unspoken thoughts in their heads. Whatever Chris' thoughts were, Jessica didn't know but she sensed his hesitancy and her expression changed to one of concern. "Come on in," she said, as she opened the door and went back inside the house.

Jessica and Erin's mom was in another room. She yelled "Hello" when they came in but went back to watching a game show on TV. Jessica led them to the kitchen where they had a round, solid oak dining table where they all sat down. Chris indeed looked troubled. Heck, he felt even more so than he looked, he was sure. When he noticed the girls opening the cabinets to grab glasses for all of them, he jumped up to help, and the other boys followed suit. He figured that would take his mind off things, at least temporarily. They took turns filling their glasses with ice and sat back down at the table. The girls retrieved a glass pitcher from the refrigerator. When someone mentioned "tea" in this neck of the woods, you could bet they meant sweet tea. This, however, could be anything from syrupy sweet to watery. Chris took a sip, and this sweet tea tasted every bit of heaven. It was just right amount of sweet without being too sugary or bitter.

"Thanks," Chris said. "This is really good tea."

Jessica looked at him and replied, "Thank you. We just made it earlier…besides, it was hot out there."

The girls then asked the boys what they were up to, so Sam went all into sharing the news about the carnival getting packed up and leaving today, just like he had with his mom. When you have news, it makes you feel important to share it. For Sam, any chance to feel important, especially in front of girls, he was going to take it. That is, of course, as long as he didn't get self-conscious about it beforehand.

"Oh, that's too bad," Erin said. "I would have liked to have gone back next weekend."

"Yeah–me too," Sam agreed, meaning that he wanted to go with her again.

"They didn't stay very long," Jessica said.

"No, they sure didn't," her sister agreed.

Chris was having a hard time thinking of anything to talk about now. He listened in as Sam, Erin and Jessica were chattering on while he was still sorting through everything on his mind. It would have been awkward but thankfully, the conversation between the participants took the focus off him and Brian, both of whom were unusually quiet in company.

Chris, getting caught up in his own mind, found himself racing from thought to thought to thought. It peaked like a tall wave breaking on the shoreline, with him finally blurting out, "Have you seen the hermit?"

It was so off-topic from the conversation the others were having, it was almost like a record screech, stopping everyone in their tracks. They all blinked and looked at him, except for Brian, who was in his own world much like Chris had been. With Chris' question, he was coming up for air, as well.

"What?" Jessica asked.

"The hermit," Brian said, jumping in. "Have you seen him?"

The girls looked at each other and then Jessica replied, "No. No, we haven't."

"How about your family?" Chris asked.

"Hmm...no, I don't think so," she said. "Why do you ask?"

"I don't know. Lately, there seem to be a lot of things that don't make sense and he seems to be at the center of it," Chris said.

"Oh...not this again," Sam said with a little bit of exasperation sneaking up into his voice.

Jessica leaned forward in her seat to listen better. "This sounds interesting. Go on."

Suddenly Chris was on the spot and wasn't sure how to proceed without looking like an idiot. He knew how he would sound. By the end of it, she would think he was crazy and wouldn't want anything to do with him. But he was pretty sure he wasn't. He just had a lot of extra memories and recent experiences he couldn't explain.

"I...uh..." he stammered.

"Do you believe in magic?" Brian said, cutting in to save the day, as well as his older brother from being in the hot seat. The girls looked at Brian as Sam sat back in his chair. "And here we go. They've been acting weird lately. I apologize on their behalf," Sam said. He tried to make it come across as a joke, but failed because the girls seemed genuinely interested in the turn of the conversation.

"I...don't know," Jessica hesitantly said.

"You mean like "magic magic"–like wizards and stuff–or that fake magic they do on stage to trick the audience?" Erin asked.

"Real magic, I guess," Chris said. "I'm not even sure what...or even if it is 'magic.'"

"What do you mean?" Jessica asked.

"Ever since we got here this summer, which granted, hasn't been very long, a bunch of strange things are going on. For instance, eating things that look like one thing and taste like another," Chris said.

"What?" Jessica asked.

"Yeah–or having memories that no one else has...or people disappearing...or..." Brian said quickly, but then shut up when all eyes turned to him.

With Brian in the hot seat, Chris returned the earlier favor since he now had his wits about him. "Yeah, the hermit invited us to eat when we saw him in the woods. His cabin looked totally out of place. Also, it looked like we all had the same thing to eat but everyone tasted something completely different. There have been other things that have happened lately that just seem...otherworldly." That wasn't quite the right word for what he was thinking, but it was the best he could come up with, on the spot, with Jessica watching with those blue eyes of hers. They really were striking when they weren't behind glasses.

"Wow, that's so strange," Jessica said, then turned toward Brian. "So, I'm guessing you asking about a horse named Rocket falls in this somewhere. I mean...you just said that you are also having memories that no one else remembers."

"Yes," Brian said, almost as a sigh of relief to get it off his chest.

Erin and Sam didn't say anything. They just sat there, looking back and forth between those that had anything to say. In truth, they really didn't know what to say or have any inclination to add anything to the conversation.

"Are you serious? This isn't some kind of joke?" Jessica asked. This time, she looked directly at Chris with a look of gravity that was borderline concern with a bit of skepticism.

"Jessica, I'm dead serious. I know I like to joke about things, but this...this is..." Chris immediately teared up and the water pooled around his eyes. He immediately felt embarrassed and had no idea that he was about to get emotional, but there it was. He wasn't crying, but he was so full of emotion he couldn't hide it as his body seemed to betray him. It was one of those things that didn't happen often, but when it did, Chris hated it. It choked him up to the point of not even being able to speak. It also happened when he was seriously angry and of course, it's never a good thing to be angry and look like you are crying, especially when dealing with a bully at school. Thankfully, he didn't have to deal with that very often. He just hated the fact that in times of extremes, it came suddenly and unexpectedly, and this time was no different.

The room grew quiet. Chris' face turned red with embarrassment and he didn't know how to get out of the situation, as if he was in a locked room and the walls were caving in. Sam was about to make another joke and it was on the tip of his tongue, but stopped short because apparently everyone else at the table understood immediately and their hearts went out to Chris.

"I believe you," Jessica said.

Her sister jumped in, saying "I do, too."

Brian looked at Chris in a different way because he had never seen his brother with tears in his eyes. His big brother, who was secretly his hero, had never shown this much vulnerability before. It was a moment of surprise, coupled with neither good nor bad feelings attached to it, just a new light he had never seen his brother in. Of course, he was still his hero, but he'd never tell him that.

"Of course I do, too. I'm in the same boat," Brian said.

Sam sighed resignedly and said, "I guess I do, too."

Chris wiped his eyes and spoke lowly, testing his voice, "Thanks."

Once he was assured his voice wouldn't crack, he

said, "I'm sorry. I didn't mean to get that way."

"It's okay, Chris," Jessica said.

Chris felt a little better hearing her words but since he hadn't expected the outburst of emotion, he was still a little embarrassed. The room grew quiet again before Jessica spoke up, saying "Well, start at the beginning and let's hear all of it."

Chris and Brian indulged her, retelling her of all the strange things that had happened since they arrived this summer–the "change" from Mrs. Willing to Mrs. Hannover, the events the night of the carnival, the fishing "help" from the hermit, the visit to his cabin...pretty much everything they could think of. They included the experience of coming to the Darling house yesterday but also the new memory of seeing them at church. When they finished, the Darling sisters and Sam sat back in their chairs, like they had just finished a long hike and were now sitting back to rest. It was a fantastic story, and they were busy digesting it.

"Well...that's...that's something," Jessica said.

Chris didn't know whether she really believed him or not–or any of them for that matter, besides Brian of course. "I know how it sounds. Believe me...I'm not crazy."

"I believe that you believe it," Jessica said, which wasn't necessarily the same as saying she believed him. She continued, "I don't think you're crazy, but it is a wild story."

"Totally," Chris agreed.

"So, now what?" Erin asked, as if she had just finished piecing a puzzle together.

"I don't know," Chris said.

"Have you told your aunt and uncle?" Jessica asked.

"No, not yet. We haven't told anyone. This is the first time that we actually spoke about any of it," Chris said.

Sam asked, "Why didn't you tell me about it?"

"Well–we tried but you didn't remember some of what happened so...you didn't really want to hear it," Brian said.

Sam opened his mouth to protest but stopped short because it was true. Jessica looked thoughtful and said, "It's so weird. You're talking about things that I should remember, but I don't."

"Imagine being us, having two sets of memory at the same time," Chris said.

"That, I could only imagine," she said.

"But it does seem that as the memories change, the earlier one seems to fade. It's like I'm having a hard time recalling the original memories," Chris said.

"Me too. In fact, I noticed that and wrote down Mrs. Willing's name on a sheet of paper that I keep in my pocket," Brian said.

Another example of quick thinking by his younger brother. "Why didn't I think of that? I should also start taking notes to keep things clear," Chris thought.

"That's a great idea, Brian," Chris said.

"What?" Brian asked.

"Writing it down so you don't forget."

"Oh–I don't know why I did it, but it does help," Brian said.

"Are you sure it's the hermit's doing?" Jessica asked.

"It's the only common thread among everything," Chris said.

"Maybe we should go confront him?" Jessica asked, questioningly.

Chris got a bad feeling about doing something like that and replied, "No, at least not yet. If he...I can't believe I'm saying this out loud...if he has the power to change memories, then who knows what he could do to us if we confronted him."

"We could tell our parents," Erin added, trying to be helpful to the conversation.

The thought of telling his aunt and uncle did cross his mind, but there was a reason he hadn't: he was afraid to bring anyone else in on this. Madame Zara didn't want any part of it, and he didn't want to bring anyone else into danger if there was any.

"No. I think we should keep this to ourselves until we know what we are dealing with," Chris said. "I hadn't planned on bringing it up today but with the way things went, I just had to get it off my chest. I do think there is real danger here."

From what he could discern from everyone else's

faces, they were all in agreement to this. It was decided that they should meet daily to compare notes. Whether they totally believed Chris and Brian didn't really matter as much as the fact that it now gave them something to do for the rest of the summer. Summers past had always brought boredom. They also decided that they would switch meeting places every other day–meeting at Sam's house the next day, followed by going back to the Darling household, and so on and so forth. With all that agreed to, the little group was formed. What answers lie ahead, they didn't know, but they were going to face this together. It gave Chris a feeling of camaraderie and that felt quite good. It also helped knowing that he would be seeing Jessica regularly, and that brought a smile to his face.

"What are you smiling about?" Jessica asked.

Chris felt like he just caught with his hand in the cookie jar. "Oh...uh...nothing. It just feels good to not face this alone and not feel so crazy," he said, thinking quickly in his response. The best part was, it was all true.

Chapter Eighteen

They went home a little later following the discussion, but not before Chris and the other boys washed their own glasses. The girls protested, saying they were guests and it wasn't a big deal but to Chris it was–so, there! At the door, with Chris leaving last, he turned to Jessica one more time and said, "Thanks for believing me."

"Well, I'm not sure I do one hundred percent, but it gives us something to do, and it's interesting, so I'm in. You could still be crazy," she said, with a smile that spoke volumes of coyness.

"Crazy? Well, that isn't so bad then, if I'm in good company," he quipped back, surprised at his own boldness.

"I guess not," she said. "'Til tomorrow then."

"'Til tomorrow," Chris repeated and smiled as he hopped off the porch. He now felt like he was walking on clouds. He felt light and full of the good kind of excitement, which was quite the change from the bad kind he'd experienced thus far this summer. Maybe it won't be a bad summer after all, he thought.

The walk home was quiet for the most part, which was fine with the boys, since they were all lost in their own thoughts. They spent the rest of the day taking notes to make sure they were all on the same page or at least, to make sure they wrote down what they remembered. Evening came and went, with Chris waking up early and excited to start the day. This was the first time he felt this way since all the chaos began. He felt refreshed and upbeat until he went downstairs and read the headlines on the local Marion Gazette morning paper. The bold letters across the top, which caught his attention and caused his heart to jump up into his throat, read "TRAVELING CARNIVAL INVOLVED IN PILE-UP ON INTERSTATE."

Chris just knew–he didn't have to read the article, but he did and with every word, his feelings of excitement shrank into despair. The article mentioned that there were fatalities and the quote from the carnival owner said it all: "The losses will be life changing."

Down deep, Chris knew that Madame Zara was dead. He didn't know how he knew this, but he knew. She didn't want to get involved but she had, and now she was gone. He also knew that the hermit was somehow involved. With every fiber of his being, he knew. Of course, he couldn't explain it, but he was absolutely certain it was true. If he could have bought a lotto ticket with the same amount of confidence he had about this, he would have won.

Now, he was regretful that he had brought anyone else into the conundrum he and his brother faced. "What have we done?" Chris thought to himself. He had looked forward to meeting everyone today to discuss plans but now, it was the last thing he wanted to do. He didn't want to get Jessica or Erin into danger, but perhaps he already had.

Brian came into the kitchen and when he saw Chris, he asked, "What's wrong?"

Chris pointed to the paper; he couldn't speak. He just shook his head and pointed. Brian picked it up and read the article. Then, with a sigh that took the wind out of his sails, he sat down hard at the kitchen table and dropped the paper back onto the table.

"She's dead," Brian said. He didn't have to identify who he was talking about; they both knew. "This isn't right," Brian continued. He was getting worked up and angry at it all. "None of this is right."

"I agree," Chris said.

"Maybe we could go talk to Pastor Williams," Brian said.

"Why?" Chris asked.

"Well, if the hermit is using magic or is supernatural, maybe Mr. Williams will know what to do. Maybe he will be protected since he is a preacher. I don't know. I just know we gotta do something," Brian said.

Chris agreed with this line of thinking but had reservations about it. "It's not a bad idea, but what if something happens to him because we talked to him?"

"Well, we gotta do something," Brian reiterated.

"I'll tell you what," Chris said, "After the girls come over this morning, we will walk to town and go speak with him. I know he usually goes to the church to clean it the day before service, so he should be there today, getting ready for Wednesday night."

"Sounds like a plan," Brian said. "If we miss him, we'll see him tomorrow night."

"Right...but I'd rather catch him alone today than have to wait 'til tomorrow night when everyone is around. I don't want to chance others listening in and hearing what we have to say. I think whatever is going on is evil and don't want anyone to become targets. I mean...we've already lost two people–one that didn't want to help but did anyway, and Mrs. Willing."

So, that's what they planned to do. They waited for the girls to show up. They didn't even mention the carnival's accident or their plans to Sam when he came down. He could detect their coolness and that something was bothering them, but he chalked it up to them being weird lately, anyway.

When the girls showed up a couple hours later, Sam invited them in and returned the favor of offering sweet tea. They accepted and they all enjoyed a glass of the refreshing beverage before they got down to business.

They all pulled out their own journals to compare notes and whatever else they had jotted down regarding the hermit and other strange things they had noticed. It became apparent that the hermit was going around and helping people in town. They only knew this because Jessica asked her mom about the hermit and her mom shared what she knew of the local gossip. Thankfully, her mom didn't ask any more questions about it. Apparently, the hermit had helped quite a few people in the village and surrounding areas, with the most random of things from pets that were sick to wells that were dry, to well...anything. There seemed to be no rhyme or reason to what he helped with. Some of the names, Chris recognized, and some he didn't. One thing was for sure–for a hermit, he sure wasn't acting like a hermit. They usually shun civilization and keep to themselves. He had been busy. "What did he gain from all the help he provided?" Chris wondered to himself.

Chris finally brought up what he had learned from the newspaper. The building excitement that had grown around the table while sharing tidbits of information suddenly diminished, like extinguishing a fire by throwing a damp blanket over it.

"Well...that's horrible," Jessica said. Her face mirrored her words with a look of surprise and horror. Everyone really had nothing more to add after that bombshell. Sam and the girls looked a little shell-shocked. It was as if the endeavor became a little more real to them than it had before. Things are like that, though–it's one thing when it's a fantasy, but quite another when it smacks you in the face. Hearing of the accident and deaths brought reality to the situation–people can die from being involved in...well... whatever was going on here in Stonemill.

"I was planning on going to talk to Pastor Williams at church, if you'd like to come," Chris said as he looked at the group. He already knew that Brian would come. With the news he had just shared, he wasn't sure how willing or interested anyone else would be in pursuing things further.

"Of course. We have to find out what's going on," Erin said.

Jessica looked at her sister then back at Chris and nodded, "I'm in."

"I guess I'm in, too," Sam said, though he didn't look like he particularly wanted to be. Nonetheless, he did agree. The group of two believers became a group of five and Chris felt joy that they decided to keep going. His joy, however, was tempered by his anxiety, which was beginning to feel like an old friend, the kind of friend you never wanted to see but that was familiar and you had to deal with them anyway.

"Just gotta call my mom to let her know," Jessica said. "She'd be upset if we left your house and something happened."

"Good idea," Chris said and pointed to where the phone was located in the living room. It was an avocado green, rotary phone, complete with a dial that you give a whirl for each digit, then have to wait until it clicks back to "0." Chris had a push-button phone at home in Florida and these rotary phones were going out of style. This one still worked perfectly, though, so there was no hurry to upgrade out here in the country.

It didn't take long for Jessica to dial the number and explain to her mom that they were heading down to the small store, just for something to do. Chris could only hear this half of the conversation so had no idea what her mom was saying. Jessica would occasionally answer "yes" and "yes, ma'am.

Apparently, it was okay because when she put the phone back on the cradle, she said she was ready to go. The boys, in turn, told Aunt Christie they were headed to the store and as usual, she just said, "Okay. Be safe."

They left the house and started down the lane that led to town. As many times as Chris had walked this path, it had never been anything new or exciting. This time, however, was different, because he had never walked to town with girls before...well, besides Sam's cousins from his dad's side. He didn't really see them that often and quite frankly, he didn't find them very interesting. But with girls, or rather, a girl that he thought was cute and interesting, it was a totally different experience. He was much more aware of the journey, in a way that didn't involve the surrounding views or the actual route itself.

"So, how are we going to bring all this up to Mr. Williams?" Jessica asked, as they walked side by side.

"I don't know. Uh...just bring it up, I guess," Chris said.

"No...I know...let's wrap a note around a rock and throw it into the church where only he will find it," Brian said, as if the conversation was the dumbest thing he'd heard all summer. To belabor the point, he said it in a deadpan manner, then followed it up with "I'm joking, of course."

"Brothers..." Chris thought, "Sometimes, they can be so awesome and then other times...well...they can be challenging." He looked at his brother and exhibiting a little frustration, said "Now is not the time to joke."

He was about to go on but then realized they were near the pond. The chance of meeting the hermit was a possibility, so he changed the topic of conversation.

"We need to be careful; we might meet the hermit along this road. We know he lives up there," Chris said as he pointed to the left toward an elevation. They couldn't see Ol' Ned's cabin, of course, due to the heavy foliage, but the group looked up in that direction and became quieter as they kept walking.

"It's so weird walking this way now," Brian said. "I always feel like I'm about to get caught or that something is watching me."

Chris felt the same. He didn't like walking to town anymore, but it was the only way there unless they took a different route, which would have turned the usual 20-minute walk into an hour-long walk. Fortunately, they didn't meet the hermit but unfortunately, the reason they felt like they were being watched was because they were. The hermit was concealed in the trees on the hill, watching them pass and smiling now. Oh, they wouldn't have seen him even if they had been looking, because he had his ways about him. Not much escaped Ol' Ned's attention…whether it be on the road, on the hill, or even in the small town.

If the boys knew how much Ol' Ned knew and what he was capable of, they probably would have just stayed at the farm and never left until their mom returned to pick them up later that summer. But they were unaware, so continued forward. Like anything, ignorance has a way of unfolding in the lives of the unsuspecting...even in the lives of those that begin to suspect. There is always a learning curve to overcome.

The group of five descended into town, making their way toward the church. The conversation had changed to one that was a bit more lighthearted, mostly about the past school year and how grateful they were that it was over.

"Yeah, I'm not looking forward to going back," Brian said, as he wrinkled his nose at the idea of the upcoming school year. "You all are in higher grades than I am, so I have a lot further to go."

What he said was true, but didn't take into account that the others had already gone through more years of school than he had. Sam pointed this out and they all had a good laugh at Brian's expense, but Brian laughed along with them. It felt good to laugh. To Chris, it seemed like it had been ages since he and Brian had laughed about something. Everything had been so somber lately and this was a good change of pace...for all of them.

The conversation then evolved to favorite movies, songs and groups...and whatever else came to mind. Everything seemed to be going great and they were just enjoying each other's company. That was, until Brian alerted everyone to black smoke billowing over Stonemill, just a few blocks away. The conversation immediately stopped as they all looked stunned, peering up at the growing cloud of darkness towering over them. The smoke looked furious and they could see embers floating in and out of the black smoke that was rising up into the air. The smoke looked to be coming from the same location they were heading. They had not confirmed it, but when Chris saw it, he knew it–in the same way that he knew that Madame Zara was dead–that the church was on fire.

Chapter Nineteen

They ran to get closer and find out what was going on. As they turned the last corner, they could see that the church was indeed on fire and it was spreading fast; the steeple was fully engulfed with fire and smoke. They could hear sirens in the distance, but they would be too late to save it. At the rate that the fire was growing, this structure would be a total loss. They also saw a small crowd, commiserate with the size of the village, beginning to form at a safe distance, to watch. It was a group of older residents who lived near the church. The town was in short supply of younger folks, as most moved to the larger communities for work and those that still lived in Stonemill weren't there this morning. Chris and the others ran the last bit and joined the group that had gathered.

"Has anyone seen Pastor Williams? His car is in the parking area," someone in the group of bystanders asked.

"No, we haven't seen him," another answered.

Chris was getting another one of those bad feelings as he watched the flames spread across the roof of the church. He felt like he had to do something. If Mr. Williams was in there, someone had to go get him. He started forward as if his legs were

211

compelled by some unknown force. He knew this was a foolish thing to do but thankfully, as he started, he saw the front doors of the church open. The entry was immediately covered by dark smoke obscuring the interior of the church. Chris saw Mr. Williams crawling out under the smoke; he looked very fatigued as if he wouldn't make it much further. Immediately, he kicked his feet into high gear and ran to help him get clear of the church. He ran over and bent down to grab Mr. Williams in order to help him up. He heard the wooden steeple begin to creak, as it started to crack. He looked up and saw the steeple swaying and wobbling, trying to stay upright. It was going to fall. His heart leapt into his throat as time seemed to slow down in incremental proportions. He could see things so clearly–the hue of the flames, the darkness and intricacies of the smoke as it changed. The paint bubbled and peeled on the sides of the church from the heat inside. He could see it all. Then time shifted back and was normal again. Behind him, Sam and Brian also came to help, causing Chris to snap out of his momentary, stunned paralysis at seeing the steeple on the verge of collapse. "Damn them!" he thought to himself angrily, out of fear for their safety. "Why did they come? They are going to get themselves killed." But thankfully, they did because it took all three of them to get Mr. Williams, who was basically dead weight at this point, to his feet. Chris got behind all of them and pushed them forward to get out of harm's way. He heard the sound of the last crack, as well as gasps from the group that was watching. He knew the steeple was now falling toward them. He gave one final push with a burst of adrenaline and heard the crash as the steeple finally collapsed. He felt the ground shake, as well as the heat and smoke envelope him from behind. The group across the way saw them and came forward to help them the rest of the way. The steeple had just missed them. Chris, himself, collapsed in a heap when he got to safety. He couldn't feel his legs and his spine felt funny from all the adrenaline that had coursed through his body. Now that the adrenaline was gone, there was a momentary "lag" as his body tried to return to normal levels. He was breathing heavily; Brian and Sam fell down beside him and Mr. Williams leaned over with his hands on his knees, coughing uncontrollably. There was soot on his face, around his mouth and nose; his eyes were bloodshot and he was breathing with difficulty, but he was alive.

Jessica came over and looked down at the boys. "I thought you were all going to die," she said angrily. Her look softened as she looked at Mr. Williams. She and everyone else who watched the event unfold knew that the boys had saved his life.

The fire department from the next town over arrived and took over the scene, unloading hoses and cordoning off an area for them to work. It didn't take them long to start spraying water on the heaping inferno. Another truck arrived from yet another town and started to help; a couple firefighters checked on Mr. Williams, who was still out of breath. They took out an oxygen tank and put a mask over his nose and mouth to assist in his breathing. An ambulance with paramedics arrived and they put him on a stretcher to check his vital signs. He looked a little worse for wear, but he'd be all right once his oxygen levels normalized, according to the lead paramedic. Chris heard one of them tell Mr. Williams that it was a good thing that he didn't burn his lungs from breathing in the hot air. It was true that he had breathed in smoke, but they didn't think it would do any lasting damage.

The small crowd that had gathered grew as the firefighters battled the blaze. It took almost thirty minutes, but the fire departments finally got the fire under control. All that was left of the church was a blackened, crisp shell of its former self. The front was now a pile of ash and most of the walls had suffered the same fate, except for the back hall behind the sanctuary. It was burned but it wasn't completely gone. The whole time the firefighters were working, the group of bystanders stood by, watching. It was the most excitement this little village had had in quite a while and would be an event they would talk about for many years to come.

The county fire inspector was the last to arrive and spoke to Mr. Williams to try and ascertain what had happened. By this time, Mr. Williams had caught his breath and his breathing and oxygen levels were more stabilized. He still looked pretty beat-up but could now talk without coughing. Thankfully, Chris was close enough to hear their conversation, if he strained to do so.

"Well, I don't know," Chris heard Mr. Williams say. "I smelled smoke coming from the front of the church, and I want to say maybe it started in the steeple, near the bell. I went to the back of the church to grab the fire extinguisher, but the sanctuary had filled with smoke so quickly, I couldn't see to make my way to the front. I tried to go out the back but the door between the sanctuary and the meeting hall had somehow closed and it wouldn't budge open."

The fire inspector was a no-nonsense kind of guy with a thick, black mustache. He took notes in a small, green, flip book as he listened. It reminded Chris of some of the police TV shows he had seen over the years.

"And then what happened?" the inspector asked.

"Well, it got so hot and it was so dark, it felt like what I'd imagine hell to be like and I thought, "This is it." But then I thought I may as well try the front door if I could get to it. I was blinded the whole way, as I ran. I know the church layout pretty well, so it wasn't that difficult to make my way in the dark. The front door felt like it was stuck, too, but thankfully, it opened at the last minute and I stumbled out, falling just outside the front doors." Mr. Williams looked deep in thought, trying to remember everything, then added, "If it wasn't for those boys helping me to my feet, I think that steeple would have fallen on me, for sure."

The pen on the notebook paused as the inspector looked up from his notes. "Boys?" he asked. Mr. Williams nodded and raised his arm to point out the boys, bringing attention to Chris, who was obviously listening in on the conversation between the two men. Chris felt immediately conspicuous about it. "Yeah– those boys over there," Mr. Williams continued. "They helped me to stand up and got me out of there in the nick of time."

"That's fortunate," the inspector said.

"Very," Mr. Williams replied.

"Ok, well, I'm done. I appreciate your time," the inspector said as he flipped closed his notebook and put it back into his pocket. I'll be back in touch if I need any more information.

"Anytime."

The inspector walked over to the boys and asked if they saw anything, which they hadn't. They explained the events from the moment they first saw smoke from down the street. It made the boys feel important, like they were part of the solution in solving some big case, but they were just standard questions so the inspector could get an idea as to what took place.

"You boys saved his life," the inspector said, finishing up his questions.

It's always nice to be recognized for hard work or for some special accomplishment. As much as Chris wanted to bask in the glory of what they had done, (because let's face it, things like that made a person feel good), he wanted to downplay their involvement as much as possible. With the idea that the hermit was possibly involved, floating around in the back of his mind, he didn't want to bring any more attention to themselves. They were already targets, he was sure, and this wouldn't help. Besides, Chris didn't really feel special about it. He imagined that anyone under the age of fifty would have done the same thing. It only happened because they were the only ones there under that age and physically capable of helping.

"No, he would have made it. We didn't really do anything," Chris said quickly. He cut off Sam, who Chris was sure was about to open his mouth to boast, or at least agree with the inspector. This would have brought more attention to them.

Sam was ready to protest but a stern look from Chris shut him up. Brian just shrugged and didn't care one way or the other.

The fire inspector noticed the exchange and didn't put any energy into having them elaborate, but it did raise a question. He asked, "Did you boys start this fire?"

The look of shock on the boys' faces at the question gave the inspector his answer. "Ok, I didn't think so, but I have to ask these questions. It's just standard," he said. "You boys have been a great help."

A short time later, Jessica's mom showed up in the blue family sedan. With the small community being what it was, it didn't take long or have far to travel. News tended to spread like wildfire (no pun intended). She parked at the edge of the road about a block away and ran up.

"Are you all okay?" she asked with concern. They all answered that they were but with the excitement of the day now gone, it left them all a little worn out. The boys weren't quite lethargic, but the adrenaline dump had taken its toll and left them with little energy remaining. They would have a good nap, here shortly, or a good night's sleep, for sure, Chris thought.

"I'm so glad," Mrs. Darling said. "When I got the

phone call telling me about the fire, I just knew you all would be here. I rushed over here as quick as I could."

Behind Mrs. Darling, Chris could see a van from the local news channel pulling up, then a reporter and cameraman got out to set up. Chris could only guess, but he was sure they were going to record a segment for the news that evening.

After Mrs. Darling made sure they were okay, she offered them all a ride home. Chris jumped on the offer immediately. He wanted to get out of Stonemill before the local news started asking questions, which was frustrating because he would have loved to be on the news. Who wouldn't? But he just couldn't risk it, nor would he allow Sam or Brian to risk it, either. If the hermit had planned on killing Mr. Williams, and the boys stopped it, Chris could only imagine what the repercussions would be. With this being such a small town, it was only a matter of time before he would find out anyway, however, there's no sense in poking the bear.

The ride home was in silence. Chris could barely keep his eyes open, with the road noise and vibration from the car nearly lulling him to sleep. With Jessica in the front seat and the other boys and Erin in the back seat with him, it made for a tight squeeze in a seat intended for three. Thankfully, they were all relatively thin and had just enough room. The ride wasn't long at all and when they got to Sam's house, Aunt Christie was waiting in the front yard. When she saw the car pull up and the boys get out, a look of relief overcame her.

Chris and the other boys thanked Mrs. Darling for the ride and said their goodbyes and that they would see the Darling girls tomorrow. At this point, with Chris being tired and numb, he realized he forgot to tell Jessica that he enjoyed hanging out with her. Oh well–lost opportunities.

"Oh, I am so glad you all are okay," Aunt Christie said. "I got a call about the church fire in town but with Bob at work, I didn't have a way to come check on y'all. I called his sister to come pick me up and I thought that might have been her pulling in when you all pulled up."

Uncle Bob's sister lived in the next town over, maybe ten minutes away. Chris had fond memories of her and her husband but realized that he hadn't seen them this summer. It was really hit or miss with spending time with them; some summers, he hadn't seen them at all.

"Maybe I can still catch her and tell her not to come," Aunt Christie said, as she turned and went back into the house, leaving the boys in the front yard.

Sam turned on Chris when they were alone, saying, "What was that about?!"

Chris didn't have a clue what Sam was getting at. It didn't help that he felt a bit sluggish and like his mind was made of mush at the moment. "What are you talking about?"

"We could have been heroes, been on TV...all that," Sam said.

"First off, I didn't do it to be a hero...and neither

did you. We just happened to be there to help and we did," Chris said.

"But we could have been famous," Sam replied.

"Don't you think I wanted to be on the news, too? Of course I did, but I didn't want to bring attention to ourselves. The hermit..." Chris started, but was interrupted.

"The hermit...hermit...hermit. It's always about that stupid hermit lately. You think he set the fire? I honestly don't think he is that bad," Sam said.

"Yes, I do think the hermit did it, or was somehow responsible for it. I don't know what he gets out of it, but it was him, all right," Chris said.

Up to this point, Brian had been quiet, but Chris and Sam heard him mutter something, as if he was thinking out loud. "He's been fishing and now he is collecting."

Chapter Twenty

This statement caused both Sam and Chris to stop talking and they turned to Brian. "What?" they said, almost in unison.

Brian was quiet for a moment longer, deep in thought while figuring out how best to describe what he meant, then snapped out of it to focus on the other boys "He is a fisherman of sorts. He fishes for things and after you bite, he collects. Think about it–he helps people or things and then something happens to them."

Brian's metaphor hit Chris like a ton of bricks. He hadn't thought of it like that before, but it made perfect sense as the idea started to connect dots in his mind. He looked at his brother and smiled. "That's pretty smart and a great way to explain it."

"Well, I wish it wasn't, because you know what that means–don't you?" Brian said, looking toward Sam.

"What?" Sam asked.

"He'll be coming for you," Brian said, with a look of gravity that gave off chills. It stopped Chris short as their focus turned toward Sam.

"Oh, come on guys. You can't be serious," Sam said. "You actually think I'm going to disappear or something? I don't even believe all the stuff you guys have been going on about. I'm only doing it because it's something to do and Erin is involved."

"Listen, the hermit offered you help with Erin, and apparently he did do something. You were even surprised about it, on some level, that Erin started giving you attention." Chris started to try to explain logically, but Sam cut him off.

"I don't want to talk about it!" he said. His voice raised in a confirmation that he was frustrated about the topic of Erin and him, but then he calmed himself and said, "It was purely coincidence."

Chris was young, but even he noticed that some people believed or saw only what they wanted to, even when evidence or logic pointed to something completely contradictory. He saw it unfolding in front of his eyes, right now. Sam didn't want to hear about it. He was getting something that he wanted–a relationship with Erin–and anything that could take that away, he wanted no part of it.

"What if you put Erin in danger?" Chris said.

"What?! I'd never do that," Sam said.

"What if you did so, not meaning to?" Brian said.

"Oh shut up! I'm done," Sam said, walking inside and leaving Chris and Brian in the front yard. Brian sighed and walked over to the road so he could look into the valley on the other side. It truly was a beautiful view. "You know, Chris, sometimes, I just like to look across this valley and think about what it would be like to be a bird flying over it," Brian said.

Chris joined his brother and looked across the valley, as well. Down the sweeping incline, he could see the last curve that went toward Erin and Jessica's house. They couldn't see their house from here because the view was obstructed by trees and another, smaller hill. Even if they were able to see it, it would only be a small dot of color, at this distance.

"Yeah, it does bring a little peace to think about things like that," Chris said.

"I'm worried about Sam," Brian said. "He doesn't believe us."

"Me, too. We'll just have to keep our eye on him," Chris said.

"Yeah, I guess it's not like we split up too often, so it shouldn't be hard to do," Brian said.

Chris felt tired, like the whole world was on his shoulders; he was totally drained and numb. He put his arm around his brother and they both trudged back to the house. When they walked in, Aunt Christie hung up the phone.

"Thank goodness. I was able to get a hold of Bob's sister and let her know you all were okay," she said as they closed the door behind them. Sam had already taken his place on the couch in the nearby living room.

"So, what happened?" she asked.

They explained everything they could from what they remembered–from seeing the smoke to helping Mr. Williams get to safety. Aunt Christie took it all in and when they finished, she commented, "Wow!

Good thing y'all were there, then. Although, you could have gotten yourselves hurt."

"It wasn't something we planned to do," Chris said. "It just sort of happened."

"I know," she said. "It just worries me how close you came to getting hurt, but I'm not mad. You all saved Mr. Williams."

She had since taken a seat at the kitchen table and spoke, thinking out loud, "I guess we won't be having church service anytime soon."

"At least not there," Chris said.

"Yeah…guess not," Aunt Christie agreed.

Chris went upstairs and lay down, following the discussion. It was late afternoon and he knew that if he went to sleep right now, he would probably wake up later, then not be able to sleep that night. He just felt like he couldn't stay awake. The excitement from events that day had finally taken its toll and he couldn't keep his eyes open any longer. He fell asleep quickly and it was a deep sleep. Thankfully, it was peaceful and full of the quiet kind of dreams that he wouldn't remember upon waking. He awoke a few hours later, with his eyes opening to see the light in the room was dim with the sun setting outside. Chris guessed it to be after 8:00, and confirmed this by looking at his wrist watch. He slept longer than he intended but he felt much better and refreshed now. He got up and realized that at some point during his extended nap, his brother came in and took a nap, as well. Not wanting to disturb him, he slipped out and went downstairs. He quickly looked out the window and saw the greyness that overtook the land during the transition between light and dark. It came with a certain, quiet excitement, as things in the country either went to sleep or woke up to take advantage of foraging at night. Like shift changeover at a factory, the night shift was taking over. Chris decided that dusk was his favorite time of day. It was a feeling like no other; he could sense the energy of change in the air.

He walked into the kitchen and living room area and saw Uncle Bob sitting in his chair, watching TV. Sam was asleep on the couch. Aunt Christie was nowhere to be seen. She was probably upstairs, he thought.

"Hey, Chris," his uncle said. "I heard about what happened. You boys did good."

For a split second, Chris was confused because he had no idea what Uncle Bob was talking about, then it dawned on him...the fire. Even though it had only been a few hours, with the nap and everything else, it felt like ages ago.

"Oh, yeah. We just happened to be there and did what anyone else would have done," Chris said.

"You'd be surprised at "what anyone else" would or wouldn't do, and you boys did. That's something to be proud of," Uncle Bob replied, turning back to watch TV.

Chris thought about what he said for a moment, then shifted gears. "Has the hermit ever asked to help you or has he done anything for you?"

Uncle Bob looked back at Chris, squinting at him. "What brought that up?"

"I don't know. He has just been on my mind lately. I hear he's been going around, trying to help people," Chris said, trying to act as nonchalantly as possible. He didn't want to raise too much attention or suspicion on why he kept asking about the hermit.

"Well–let me think," Uncle Bob said. "As a matter of fact, he did ask once but I turned him down."

"What was it?" Chris asked.

"It was shortly after he asked if he could fish at the pond. I was out in the field near there and you know that old broken-down tractor that's out there?"

"Yeah."

"Well, he said he could fix it and...I don't know...I just turned him down. I didn't like the idea of owing him anything nor do I like the idea of someone doing something that I can very well do myself. It's just that I haven't had time to get out there to tinker on it."

"If he ever offers again, I wouldn't accept," Chris said.

"Why do you say that?"

"I don't know. I think there are strings attached with all his 'good deeds.'"

Before the conversation went any further, headlights appeared in the front yard and shone through the living room window, notifying those inside that someone had arrived. Chris went closer to the window to peek out. The two-tone tan truck was the only vehicle out there and Aunt Christie was getting out. Chris learned after she came inside, that when Uncle Bob got home from work, she apparently took the truck to see the damage at the church.

"It's horrible," she said. "Absolutely horrible. It's one thing to hear of it but it's another thing to actually see it."

"How's Pastor Williams? Have you heard anything about him?" Uncle Bob asked his wife.

"Yeah. I stopped by Mrs. Mable's house since she lives close to the church and has an ear to the ground on everything. He's doing better, but still shook up."

"I can imagine," Uncle Bob said.

"I can too, but don't want to," Aunt Christie immediately replied. "Just never know what will happen or when it's your time."

"Or just get taken out of existence, like that one store lady" Chris thought to himself. He couldn't remember her name at the moment, but he had it written down in his journal upstairs. In fact, all the memories of that lady were fading.

"By the way–I thought I blew a tire on the way home," Aunt Christie said.

Uncle Bob moved to get up, with a concerned look across his face. "What happened?" he asked.

"Oh, it's fine. That hermit that likes to fish at our pond helped me," she replied.

As soon as the words left her lips, Chris felt his

knees almost buckle at the news. He grabbed onto the kitchen table and lowered himself into the chair, which required great concentration so he wouldn't just fall on the floor from surprise.

"What..." Chris began. "What did he do?"

"Are you okay?" she asked. "You look pale. Are you feeling sick?"

"No. I'm fine; just a crazy day. What did he do?" Chris said quickly to get back on topic.

Uncle Bob came and sat down at the kitchen table, as well, to hear the story.

"Well, I was near the pond when I heard a pop and the truck shook like I blew a tire. Thankfully, I wasn't going very fast. Let's see...I then pulled to the side and got out. It was getting dark and I could have sworn it was a flat tire. As I was going around the truck to see which tire it was, the hermit came out of nowhere, which scared me at first because I wasn't expecting anyone," Aunt Christie said.

"What was he doing out there?" Uncle Bob asked.

"He told me that he was fishing at the pond and heard the pop, then asked if I wanted help. I said "sure" and he walked around to see which tire, then stooped down at the front passenger tire. I couldn't see what he was doing because I was still on the driver's side, but he wasn't down there very long. When I began to walk around to his side, he stood up, holding a thick stick and told me that was the problem. Apparently, I hit a stick in the road, and it got caught in the tire. It's strange, though...I didn't see anything in the road and it sure felt like a flat tire," Aunt Christie said, finishing the story.

"Well, I'm glad you're okay and that it worked out, then," Uncle Bob said. "I'm not sure we could afford a flat tire right now."

"I know. That's exactly what I was thinking to myself, on the side of the road, there," Aunt Christie replied.

It was a flat tire, though, Chris thought to himself. Whatever the hermit did, he fixed it, but it was a flat tire. He was sure of it. Then, as if the situation couldn't get any worse, he realized there were now two people that he and Brian had to keep their eye on.

Chapter Twenty-One

The next day, the group of five met again at the Darling house. Most of them made sure to bring their journals but when it was time to compare notes, Sam didn't have his. He really wasn't taking this seriously at all. Like he had said, he was really only involved because Erin was and that's all there was to it.

"Sam, you were supposed to bring yours," Brian said.

"It's no big deal. Mine is about the same as yours. I'll have it tomorrow," Sam replied.

The look that Brian gave Sam spoke volumes of disapproval. "But that's just it. That's why it's important to bring the notes. Yours might be slightly different than mine. You really should take this more seriously," Brian said, ending the conversation. Chris looked at them, then at the girls and shrugged his shoulders. At least the girls still seemed interested. Chris thought going forward, he should make sure that everyone, including Sam, had what they were supposed to have. The boys had worn backpacks today and Chris just assumed that Sam brought his notes.

As they compared notes, Jessica wrote in her spiral notebook. Chris could see the prettiest handwriting in purple ink, complete with flowing and large loops in the characters. Erin had a small, diary-type book that, at one time, she was going to use just for that purpose, but never followed through. Now, it was the handiest thing she could find to take notes with. Brian had a memo pad and Chris…well…he just had loose leaf paper in a three-ring binder that he used in English class the past year, which he barely passed.

They sat around the Darlings' kitchen table and were trying to figure out how to go about comparing notes. Sam sat by Erin and looked over her shoulder at her notes. They started off the meeting talking about yesterday's events at the church and comparing what everyone saw or experienced. There was nothing peculiar about any of it except that the building that they were all so familiar with was now gone, which in and of itself, brought about its own type of peculiarity.

Chris told them about Aunt Christie's run-in with the hermit and that caught Sam's attention. "What? Why didn't you say anything to me about this before?" he asked.

"You were asleep on the couch, and besides, you don't seem to care about what's going on anyway."

"Yeah, but it's my mom we're talking about now."

Retorting quickly and without thinking, Chris said, "So? You didn't care about your own dealings with the hermit but now you're concerned about your mom's safety?" As soon as the words escaped his lips, he knew that Sam's little secret about Erin would come to light.

"What?" Erin asked, as she looked back and forth between Sam and Chris "What do you mean 'dealings' with the hermit?"

Sam's face turned red with embarrassment and anger. "Nothing. It's nothing," he replied.

The explanation of "nothing" didn't answer the question to Erin's satisfaction, whose face, by this time, reflected a look of suspicion at all the boys. "What's going on?"

Jessica, too, shared a look that mirrored her sister's expression. Up to this point, they had never spoken to the Darling sisters about Ol' Ned asking Sam if he would like help with Erin. It was one of those things that they knew wouldn't end well if brought up. In his haste, coupled with frustration with Sam, Chris had accidentally let it slip.

Chris saw Brian rock back into his chair with a big smile on his face, staying out of the conversation, as if he knew what was about to go down. It wasn't going to be pretty but to be honest, Chris had to agree with what he imagined Brian to be thinking. It wasn't that he particularly enjoyed his cousin having a hard time, but he figured it wouldn't hurt for him to be knocked down a peg or two, especially since Sam didn't seem to take any of this Ol' Ned stuff seriously.

"No…really…it's nothing…" Sam attempted, but was cut off.

"I want to know," Erin said.

In the end, Sam knew he would have to tell and took a deep sigh to steady himself, "Well…you see...uh..."

"It's okay. You can tell us," Erin said, but that assurance didn't seem to help, as Sam became more awkward in delivering his explanation.

"The night we all met at the carnival...well...we were hanging out," Sam began.

"And?" Erin said, to help him along. Everyone else at the table was silent. The boys were awaiting the delivery of a possible bombshell and the girls were just intrigued about this missing information. They had the feeling they weren't getting the whole story but were about to.

"Well...I...you know I enjoy hanging out with you," Sam said. "And I really like you."

"And I like you, too" Erin said.

"And Ol' Ned was there, and he asked me if...you know...if I wanted help getting you to like me..." Sam said, with his eyes downcast.

"What?!" Erin said.

"Well, I didn't think it would hurt. He seemed like a regular, old guy to me. I didn't know about all this other stuff, and I was like, "What could it hurt?" So, I said "yes"...and...uh...that's when you turned around and asked if I wanted to go together," Sam said.

Silence filled the room and the feelings of togetherness deflated like air leaving a balloon through a pinhole. It was almost tangible. The moment lingered as Erin tried to process what she had just heard. "So...let me get this straight," she started,

"You mean to tell me that I was 'made' to like you, or some sort of magic happened to make me like you?"

"I honestly didn't think it would happen," Sam said, defensively, "but then it did."

"Why didn't you tell me before? In fact, why didn't any of you say anything about this before now?" Erin asked. Chris was afraid of the direction this seemed to be heading. He could tell she wasn't quite angry, yet, but was getting wound up. It was similar to how the area around volcanoes tremored, leading up to a final eruption.

No one had an answer, but Sam said, "I didn't want you to get mad and I didn't know what to do. I mean…I wanted to tell you but didn't know how and it never seemed like the right time." That was the truth, but truth, as good as it is, doesn't always help make things good. It can hurt and be just as sharp as any sword, with the pain that comes from it.

Erin looked at Sam, then at everyone else around the table and made a decision. She closed her book and stood up. "I don't want to do this anymore. Jessica, you are more than welcome to continue but I don't want any part of it anymore."

Without saying goodbye, she walked away, to her room at the back of the house and shut the door behind her. And just like that, the spell, or whatever it had been, was broken. It seemed that Erin didn't just not like Sam anymore but no longer liked the whole group, excluding her sister.

Jessica watched her sister leave the room. Everyone around the kitchen table remained silent in the aftermath, taking in what just happened. Jessica looked at Chris and said, "I think y'all should probably go home."

There was no emotion in Jessica's face and Chris couldn't tell if that was good or bad. He wasn't sure if they were going to have another meeting or not. Chris hadn't expected the fallout to be this way but as usual, nothing rarely works out as one expects it to. He expected it to be just a bump they'd get over, but not something that would end the group.

"Uh...sure," Chris said, as he grabbed his binder and stuffed it down into his backpack. By this time, Sam had quickly packed and left the house, mumbling something, but no one could make out what he was saying. Chris noticed that his eyes were tearing up and he suspected that he hurried out to avoid more embarrassment from everyone seeing him cry. He guessed he said something along the lines, "I'll see you at the house." Chris looked at Brian, who just shrugged when their eyes met, then they both slowly got up from the table.

"I'm sorry about everything," Chris said.

"It's okay. Sometimes weird things happen here, apparently," she replied, with a slight smile that eased the tension between them.

This gave Chris confidence enough to ask if she would like to meet tomorrow, but she said she didn't think that would be a good idea, at least not for a while. She didn't want to leave her sister hanging and would like to get her to come around first. It wasn't bad news, but it wasn't great news, either, because

Chris had a sneaking suspicion that for all intents and purposes, this group and its purpose was over and done with. With the church gone and no weekly schedule with which he was sure to see them, he wasn't sure when he would be able to ask them if they wanted to continue.

A couple of minutes later found Chris and Brian walking home. It was still mid-morning, and the sun was bright. The sky was blue, without a single cloud in sight. It was breezy, so it wasn't muggy or hot. When the brothers were down the lane, about to go around the curve that would cause the Darling house to disappear from view, Brian spoke up, "Well, that sucked."

"Yes, it did. Now it's just us again," Chris said. Without having the others to help make observations and compare notes about all the odd things happening, Chris' anxiety was returning. He felt like he was traveling up a mountain alone, with a long way to go.

"So, with Erin free, do you think that Ol' Ned could help me out with her?" Brian said, almost laughing at the idea.

Chris knew he was joking but it was not the right time. "Not funny," Chris replied.

"Sure, it is. You just gotta be in the right frame of mind to appreciate it," Brian bantered back, but when Chris remained silent, Brian continued, "I wasn't being serious. That's how I handle hard times–with humor."

"I know," Chris said and then with a smile, he continued, "Besides–you don't need the hermit's magic. You can use your own but I think it's more of a repellent, so it might not work."

"Oh–very funny," Brian said.

Chris realized it was almost therapeutic to joke, as it did take his mind off what they were facing. And anything that would take his mind off that was a good thing.

"Do you think they will come around?" Brian asked, nodding back in the direction they came from.

"I don't know. I guess Erin is upset because she felt like she was an object, and no one likes that. And Jessica–I don't know. I have no idea how girls think or what they like or...anything, really," Chris admitted, truthfully.

Brian smiled. "Yes, that's kind of obvious and I think your powers of repellent are just as strong as mine–maybe even stronger," to which both boys chuckled as they continued to walk. They came up to the farm on the right and strangely, the little dog that always came out to greet (or rather, bark) at them hadn't come today, neither this morning nor now. They saw old farmer Andrews sitting on his front porch, so Chris waved at him and raised his voice to say "Hello" and ask, "Hey Mr. Andrews! Where's your dog? I haven't seen him today."

The farmer waved back and asked, "What?"

"Your dog–where is he?" Chris asked again.

"We don't have a dog," Farmer Andrews yelled back, "Have you seen one hanging out here?"

"Oh...my mistake. I thought you had one," Chris replied. Farmer Andrews just waved, acknowledging Chris' response.

Chris knew he wasn't mistaken and both Brian and he knew that the little dog was gone, just like the Darling horse. Like his memories of the store lady were becoming fainter by the day, his memories of the horse were fading, as well. Chris wondered what Ol' Ned did to help Farmer Andrews, though it was pointless to even ask because no one would remember the little dog. They were rudely forced back into gravity of the situation. Chris couldn't help but wonder about how many times something like this had happened in his life or in the lives of others. Things just happening and no one remembering. It was a scary thought that just seemed to grow scarier with each new and strange encounter.

"This day just keeps getting better," Brian said, as they continued.

"Let's hope we don't have any more surprises," Chris said. "I think I've had enough for one day.

Unfortunately, though, they had one more surprise waiting for them when they got home. Sam wasn't there.

"You boys are back early," Aunt Christie said when they came through the front door.

"Yeah, it didn't go like we expected," Chris said, as he sat down at the small kitchen table. Aunt Christie was washing dishes, humming a song as she took a break to look out the window over the sink every so often.

"What do you see out there?" Chris asked.

"Oh…nothing really. I just like to look out there. Sometimes there's cows in the pasture. Sometimes horses. Every once in a while, I'll see deer," she said. "It's amazing what you'll find if you're patient and look long enough."

Chris supposed that to be true, but every time he looked out there, he never saw anything interesting…well…not interesting to him. Just more of the same old pasture that he saw last time he looked.

"Where's Sam?" Aunt Christie asked when she had finished with the dishes.

"He's not here?" Chris asked.

Chapter Twenty-Two

"No. He wasn't with you?"

"He left the Darlings' place before we did. We figured he was here already," Chris said.

"What happened?" Aunt Christie asked.

Chris explained what occurred without getting in the weeds with all the details. He said that Sam and Erin had broken up over a miscommunication and Sam left in a hurry, to get out of there. Aunt Christie was a little concerned, but she wasn't alarmed. This was a small, rural community, not some large city. There hadn't been a report of an abduction ever taking place in the area, but it wasn't totally out of the realm of possibility since there's always the first time for everything. So, she was a little worried but wasn't freaking out…yet. "And you boys didn't see him on the way back?"

"No, ma'am," they both replied.

"He might have just wanted to be alone for a bit," Brian said. "That's what Erin did–she went to her room to be alone. Maybe it's the same thing here."

"Hmm...maybe...but that doesn't seem like him, "Aunt Christie said. "Why don't you boys go looking for him. I'll stay here for a bit to see if he comes back. Check all the places you think he'd go, but I want you boys back in one hour, though–no more."

The only place that Chris could think of was maybe he had gone to their old fort, Gopher's Gulley, so that's the first place they decided to check first. It took about ten minutes to walk to there, but there was no sign of him. They then went to the pond, worried that Ol' Ned might still be there, as he always seemed to be at the pond. Neither Ol' Ned nor Sam were there. They checked the barn on the way back and nope–nothing. Sam was nowhere they thought he'd be. After an hour passed, they trudged back to the house. The front door was unlocked, but this time when they went in, no one was home, which was very odd. Chris looked and there wasn't a note left for them–also out of character for Aunt Christie. Brian started to get fidgety. "Where are they?" he asked, his voice full of concern. "What if something happened to them?

Chris didn't want to give it any thought because he knew that if he did, his imagination would run wild and the fear would be unstoppable. So, he told his brother to shut up. "She probably went looking for him, herself," Chris said, making something up–anything up–to change the subject. He knew how unlikely that would be for Aunt Christie, though. She was the type of person who would have done what she said, and she said that she would wait for them, so she should have been here.

Chris looked outside and then at his watch; it was just after noon. He turned to his brother and said, "The only other place I can think of that we haven't checked, is in town. Let's leave a note and we can walk there to see if that's where they are."

Brian just nodded. His face was a shade of white, probably from his imagination ravaging him inside, Chris thought. Chris stopped, grabbed Brian by his shoulders and told him that it was going to be okay, while secretly trying to convince himself that it was. Chris took a sheet of paper from the three-ring binder in his backpack and wrote a quick note.

"Aunt Christie: We went into to town to look for Sam. We won't be gone long.

Love you, Chris"

Chris looked at his penmanship and sighed. His handwriting had always embarrassed him. It would be a wonder if she, or anyone for that matter, could read it, Chris thought to himself. He left the note in the middle of the kitchen table so anyone coming through the front door would see it upon entering. A few minutes later, they were on the road to town and Chris asked himself out loud, "Where would I go if I were Sam?" It was a rhetorical question and more or less spoken aloud because he thought it would help jog his brain to think better.

"Oh, no..." Brian said, his voice shaking.

Brian's voice caused Chris to turn and give him his undivided attention. "What?" Chris asked.

"What if he wanted to fix things between him and Erin?" Brian said. As soon as the words left Brian's mouth, Chris knew why Brian's voice wavered with concern.

"He couldn't have..." Chris started, but he knew

that Sam very well could have and the more he thought about it, would have. Sam didn't think the hermit was that bad and if he believed Ol' Ned helped him before, what was to stop him from believing that Ol' Ned would help him now. Sam had gone to go to see the hermit.

They were too far along to go back to the house to leave another note. They had to go now, hopefully in time to stop Sam from doing something stupid. Chris turned toward Brian, "You have to go back to the house."

"What?! Why?" Brian protested.

"What if something bad happens? You need to go back to let Aunt Christie know where I went."

"Chris, this isn't a good idea. We need to go together," Brian said.

"Think about it. If Ol' Ned really is bad like we think he is, we need someone to stay behind to tell everyone," Chris said.

"Right…but that will only work if they remember you," Brian said.

"Listen, we don't have time. Go back to the house," Chris said.

Deep down, Brian knew that Chris was right, and it was the best course of action. If something happened to them both, no one would know. He still didn't like it.

Brian turned to go, but stopped and looked back. "I love you," he said.

"I love you, too," Chris replied. It was a somber and serious moment. There was no telling what would happen next but, in their family, they always told each other how they felt because they never knew if it would be the last time. Chris turned and ran into the forest, leaving his brother behind. Brian lingered a bit on the side of the road, watching his brother disappear into the brush, before turning and heading back to the house.

Chris tore up the side of the hill, heading to where he remembered Ol' Ned's place was located, with his feet gliding across the ground. He was too afraid to stop or slow down and was going too fast for the terrain. He tripped halfway up and would have rolled, but thankfully he was able to grab a small tree branch, which kept him on his feet. Chris took a moment to catch a couple of deep breaths before he moved ahead again, like a bat out of hell. Thankfully, the sun still peeked through the trees so it wasn't as scary. Had it been night, being in the woods would have been totally different. Chris didn't have time to think on that little bit of good fortune, though. His mind raced across a broad spectrum of possibilities in what he would find waiting for him. As he got closer, he heard and felt what he thought was a sonic boom that caused the ground to shake as the sound wave passed him by. At least, that's what he thought it was. In Florida, where he lived, there was a nearby Air Force base where the jets would often break the sound barrier. This wasn't exactly like what he experienced when the jets flew overhead, but it was similar.

He picked up the pace and soon, he was in the

nearing the hermit's cabin. It looked exactly like it did the last time he was there. Ol' Ned was standing in the middle of the clearing in front of cabin, looking over the fire pit, with his back toward Chris. Without turning he spoke, "Ah...young Chris. What brings you way out here...by yourself."

Chris stopped short and looked around. "How did you know it was me?" Chris asked.

"Come now," Ol' Ned said, still with his back toward Chris. "We don't have to play these little games anymore. I know everything that happens in these woods...and that little village of yours."

Chris didn't know what to say. He was momentarily speechless because he didn't know how to respond to a comment like that. Then, he saw Sam's backpack near the fire in front of Ol' Ned. This confirmed Chris' suspicion that his cousin had come here. "I've come looking for my cousin Sam. Where is he? I know he was here."

Ol' Ned's shoulders shook, as if he were laughing silently to himself. He slowly turned around and his eyes were a bright, unnatural blue–almost neon–as he looked over at Chris. Ol' Ned smiled a wide, toothy smile that seemed too large for his face. This time, Chris knew it wasn't the sunlight coming through the trees, playing tricks with him. The hermit's face was unnatural, and not just that his smile didn't reach his eyes, like he had noticed before. It was like a mask...and Chris was afraid to see what was underneath. The hermit raised his hand to wipe his mouth, like a person would do after having a meal.

"Your cousin? Oh, you just missed him," he said, almost like he was letting Chris in on a private joke that he didn't understand.

Chris' legs started to tremble, only amplifying his feelings of fear. Maybe he shouldn't have come alone, after all, but at least his brother wasn't in danger.

"Where did he go? I didn't see him while I was on my way up," Chris said.

"I expect you didn't. He's gone."

"Wha...What did you do to him?"

"Let's just say...he was full of energy...and I really like that kind of energy, the kind I get from people," Ol' Ned said. His electric-blue eyes took on a sinister look as he gave Chris complete focus of his attention.

Chris' head suddenly and unexpectedly started throbbing with pain. It pounded as if a migraine was coming on with full force. It was enough to cause his stomach to churn and he thought he was going to be sick, which right now, was neither the time nor place.

"Are you okay, Chris?" Ol' Ned's voice carried no warmth or concern, as he came closer. It seemed he was enjoying Chris' discomfort, like it was a delicacy. His eyes still had a slight otherworldly glow, but it wasn't quite as bright as it was a moment ago. They pulsed as the intensity of color waned.

Chris stumbled backward, not wanting the hermit to get closer than he already was. His vision started to spin, and he had a hard time staying upright.

"It's easier if you don't fight it," Ol' Ned offered. "You should let me help you. Would you like help?"

Chris crouched and muttered "No. Stay away from me."

"Suit yourself. It's only a matter of time before you will want my help. This town and those inhabitants are slowly becoming mine. There's really nothing you can do about it."

Chris looked for Sam's backpack, but it wasn't there any longer, as if it suddenly disappeared. Trying to maintain his sense of the world, he asked "Where's Sam's bag? Where did it go?"

"Sam who?" The hermit asked, with an amused smile. It was a smile that not only did not touch his eyes, but also spoke volumes about an inside story to which only he was privy.

"You know who I'm talking about," Chris said.

"Maybe. But then again, maybe not. Things have a way of changing around here," the hermit replied.

Chris' head, still reeling from the pain, exploded with a different kind of pain as new memories rushed into his mind. It was as if someone had come along and hit him over the head with a club. He was seeing stars and felt dizzy as his mind shifted. This had happened a couple times already this summer, when two conflicting memory sets were fighting for domination in his mind. But this…this was the worst yet, and almost unimaginable. The new memories that started seeping in reflected a life totally without Sam. Almost thirteen years of memories were moving aside at light speed, racing out of his mind; he had remembered when Sam had been born but it was all slipping away. New memories came–memories of an annoying little cousin named Tabitha, who was only nine, as well as a whole host of other changes. And his brother…his brother!

The shock of it all immediately brought back a laser-like focus. He gained control of himself to the point that it seemed as if the world had stopped spinning. He looked once more at Ol' Ned. "My brother…" he said.

"Ah–yes. I told you. You may be back before too long, looking for help," the smile on his face widening, as if he knew the inevitable.

Chris took off and flew back the way he had come. Amazingly, he was traveling faster, and it had nothing to do with the downslope of the hill. He was full of fear at what awaited him back at Aunt Christie's house. He only gained speed and never slowed. Chris was on autopilot at this point, and his mind kicked into higher gear, blocking out all peripheral information and only doing what it needed to keep him going and keep him upright. He came out of the woodline like a rocket. His chest was heaving and lungs burning, but his desire to get home buffered the temptation to slow down or stop. He was breathing so heavily and his heart pumping so hard that he developed a stitch under his right ribcage, as his lungs worked as bellows moving mass amounts of air. Chris came around the first curve and saw the familiar road in front him. This moved in a gradual slope up to the second and final curve that he had to pass in order to get home. He could see the house off to the left, higher on the hill. A moment later, he was around the second curve and could see the dirt driveway coming up fast. He did not slow down until he collided with the front door, rushing inside. The force at which the front door opened surprised Aunt Christie, who jumped in her seat at the kitchen table when he burst in. Tabitha, who looked to be about nine or ten years old, sat in the seat next to her, equally surprised.

Aunt Christie could see that Chris was breathing heavily and his face was a deep shade of red. It scared her, as she had never seen him in such a state. She was about to ask if he was okay, but she didn't have a chance because Chris raced up the stairs, calling out for Brian. He rushed into Sam's (or rather, Tabitha's) room, looking for Brian. The room looked nothing like what he remembered when it was Sam's room and the new memories of this room started to fill his mind. What was once a light blue room with navy trim was now a light pink one with white trim. It wasn't something that he expected, and it caused him to take a moment to think. He also discovered that in this new reality, or whatever it was, he and Brian didn't stay in this room during the summers. They shared the guest bedroom downstairs, letting Tabitha have her own room and privacy. Reversing in his steps, he headed back downstairs, yelling for his brother. He met Aunt Christie at the bottom of the stairs who had followed him to see if he was okay. Tabitha was there, too, and piped up, "What were you doing in my room?"

Chris ignored both of them as he passed them. He ran to the hall leading to the guest bedroom that was at the back of the house. The door was closed, and Chris was praying...hoping...crying...with all of his might, about what he would find when he opened the door. "Brian! Bri..."

Chris opened the door and walked in the room, only to find that he was the only occupant that had been staying there. Brian's stuff was nowhere to be seen and the memories without Brian became stronger. Aunt Christie came to the door, "Are you okay?"

"Where's Brian?" Chris asked. "I can't find him."

His eyes filled with tears from fear and shock.

"Don't you remember?" she asked quietly and with a voice that was gentle and full of concern. Even her eyes teared up a little as she asked. Chris shook his head repeatedly, in denial of the new memories that were taking over his mind. He didn't have to hear her say it but when she did, it confirmed what he already knew. "He passed away last summer. You don't remember?"

Chapter Twenty-Three

Chris did remember, or at least was aware of the new memories forming in his mind. The old memories were still fresh, which only brought shock and pain.

"What?" Chris said, in a weak voice, while holding back tears. He felt compelled to say something, and needed further confirmation that this nightmare was real.

Aunt Christie continued to look at him with an uncertain, but concerned face. Tabitha was in the door behind her. She had a blank look on her face that gave away nothing except for maybe a little intrigue, as she had never seen Chris in such a state.

"The rafting accident at the pond last year. I have no idea why we let you boys build that thing. It looked unsafe. Brian wasn't a great swimmer and when we realized something was wrong, it was too late. Don't you remember?"

Hearing her say the words rammed home with the force of the new reality that Chris lived in. His mind screamed "No!" and it would have been deafening if anyone could have heard it. The incident at the pond…yes, he remembered. The pond was deep where the raft went down, and Brian had somehow gotten caught up in it as it went down. He wasn't a strong swimmer and by the time anyone realized he wasn't coming up, it was too late. Chris wasn't close to him at the time, and in situations like that, every second counts. They tried to perform CPR when they got him to the shore, but Brian never came back.

Chris remembered the other memory, as well–the one with Sam in it. Sam was close to Brian and noticed that his foot had gotten caught. Before swimming to safety, he helped untangle Brian and they both swam to the shore. Now that Sam was gone, seemingly erased from existence, he couldn't have been there to help save Brian.

Along with these new memories were memories of a troubled school year since Brian's passing. The trauma had left him in a state of constant depression and the only reason that he had come to southern Illinois this summer was because his mom didn't want him to be alone while she was at work. He was so apathetic about everything that he just went with it. It was like looking at some strange image of yourself in a mirror, waving at you, but you weren't really waving. It was him, but yet it wasn't. The more the concreteness of this new reality took hold, the more his mind fought it. "No! I won't accept this!" Chris thought to himself. "I have got to get out of here." He felt the walls of the room close in on him. His breath became shallow and his mind was panicking. "I've got to get outside. I need air."

Aunt Christie could see his distress and stepped forward to give him a hug, but he pushed past her and Tabitha, into the hall. He didn't give any explanation. He just had to leave the house and these...people. Like seeing another version of himself in the mirror, this wasn't the Aunt Christie he knew. And Tabitha? He had no idea who she was except for the new memories that told him. He continued on down the hallway, toward the door. Chris heard Aunt Christie raising her voice, telling him to stop. He just couldn't. He had always minded her before but again, this wasn't his Aunt Christie.

Chris opened the front door and took off down the road again. He didn't know where to go, just that he had to go somewhere to think. He thought about maybe going and seeing Jessica but unfortunately, that wasn't an option because the new memories told him that they hadn't really developed a friendship. He was all alone in this…new…life. He felt cornered and trapped.

"Maybe I could ask the hermit for help…to maybe fix it," he thought, but knew that wasn't an option. Ol' Ned–whatever he was–was a trickster and any help he provided, the price was worse. He thought of Stonemill and decided to go there as a last resort. There was nothing in particular he planned to do once he got there, but he had to go somewhere. Everything here reminded him of Brian, which felt like a knife being twisted at every turn. Going to Stonemill would have some more twists of that very same knife, but at least he wouldn't be at a house or farm filled with the memories that he couldn't bear to face.

With the tears streaming from his eyes, he was surprised he was even able to see the road, but again, he knew the way like he knew the back of his hand. Halfway there, the tears let up and stopped altogether, but the feeling of despair remained…and it was a heavy burden to bear. He stumbled to the outskirts of the village and the little hill that overlooked it. He felt so hopeless. He honestly didn't know how much more he could go. The memories of depression were becoming more real to him now, and combined with the shock of everything, it was twofold and it was worsening by the second.

It was all so overwhelming and he felt lightheaded. He needed to sit down. Chris saw the Catholic church in his peripheral vision, but didn't think he had the strength to even get to the front door. He collapsed off to the side of the road, in the church yard. It was afternoon by this time. The sky had turned grayish and overcast, which Chris only minutely noticed because it had been sunny and blue when he left the farm 20 minutes ago. The winds were also picking up; a summer storm must be on the way, but Chris felt nothing in regard to it. In a way, he thought, "Sure, why not? Just let it pour. It would fit this day perfectly. It's absolutely the worst day of my life, so why not let it rain to really drive it home?"

Chris was spent. He was tired, had no one to turn to and felt like he had nowhere to go. "I give up. I just want to die. I can't take this. The memories of Brian and his loss are so real and painful," Chris thought to himself.

"What's wrong, Chris?"

The voice startled Chris, as he hadn't seen anyone nearby and thought he was alone. He looked up to see Father Bishop standing over him. Chris tried to speak but that damn emotion choked him up again. He couldn't get a word out. The priest could clearly see that Chris was in distress and he bent down to help Chris up.

"Come on. Let's go inside. There's a storm coming and there's no sense staying out here to get wet," he said. Chris heard him but at the same time, couldn't comprehend anything being said. He allowed Father Bishop to help him up and help him inside the church, with an arm around his shoulder. They made it inside right as the deluge hit. Chris could comprehend enough to see and hear the lightning and thunder build. The storm, strangely enough, reminded Chris of that carnival night when he last saw...now he couldn't remember her name. Father Bishop sat Chris down in the pew closest to the door and sat down in the one in front of him so he could sit at an angle and talk face-to-face with Chris.

It took a few minutes for Chris to calm down. The thunder shook the building and Father Bishop dawdled on about how strange the storms had been lately. Finally, he turned to Chris and asked if he'd like to talk about whatever was going on. Chris remained silent, not sure about how to begin or even what to say, without sounding absolutely crazy.

"How's your cousin Sam and brother Brian?" Father Bishop asked.

The last sentence struck Chris like a semi-truck. He almost fell off the pew and to the floor in surprise. "Sam and Brian?" Chris choked out.

"Yes, you all are always together, so it's a little surprising to see you by yourself," the priest continued.

"You remember them?" Chris whispered, looking at the priest like he had just become a bar of shining gold.

Chris' question caused Father Bishop to lean back and then look off into another direction, as if seeing something deep in his thoughts or peering at something that Chris couldn't see. "Oh…I see. Things have changed." And then he looked back at Chris and smiled a gentle, knowing and warm smile. "Chris, I think it's time for you to tell me what's going on."

Father Bishop's eyes twinkled, and Chris was momentarily dumbfounded. He believed that the priest knew all about what was going on or at least, how or why it had all happened. He also knew, somehow, that Father Bishop would believe him, no matter how crazy his story sounded. Chris began to explain, his voice raspy from the pure emotion, then cleared his throat and began again. He started from the beginning. He talked about the Ol' Ned, the hermit–when they met at the pond and the experience at his cabin; the strange occurrences at the store; the disappearance of…Mrs. Willing, whom he barely remembered now; Rocket the horse; the little group of friends that met to discuss the strange things happening in town. He told of how Sam ran into the woods to seek help from Ol' Ned and that something had happened…and how new realities seemed to form and replace the current, familiar reality. He spoke of how his memories were battling one another in his mind–like two lines converging with one becoming less visible over time, until it finally disappeared. He explained how he was afraid of losing the memory that he had of his brother, the one where he was alive just a couple hours ago. It took him the better part of an hour to get it all out in the open. The storm raged outside, and Father Bishop never interrupted while Chris talked. It seemed to Chris that the priest had all the time in the world and was listening attentively, taking it all in. He just nodded or asked the regular, prodding questions like, "What happened then?" or "What did you do next?" As Chris explained, he calmed down and didn't feel so overwhelmed. It felt so good to talk and get it all off his chest, and also to have someone believe what he was saying. He had not realized just how heavy it all was. It felt as if the weight of the world had been lifted off his shoulders. When he was done, he sighed. It was a relief like no other he had ever experienced.

The priest took it all in, until the end. It seemed to Chris that the priest seemed to get more and more excited as the story went on–not in an alarming way, but as if putting a puzzle together and finding the missing pieces that had eluded you from the start. The thrill of the final piece being added showed plainly on Father Bishop's face.

"I'm so grateful that you shared that with me, Chris. I imagine it's been a long, strange summer despite only having been a few weeks so far," Father Bishop said.

The priest's eyes weren't dark anymore. Chris had never gotten close enough to see the exact color of his eyes, but they had always appeared dark. Now, they seemed to have lightened some. It wasn't a quick change and had Chris not been so close, he wouldn't have noticed the subtle change.

"Do you think you could introduce me to Ol' Ned?" the priest asked.

"Well, sure I can, but what are you going to do? I don't think he is..." Chris stumbled for the appropriate words because he felt stupid saying it, "from this world."

"Hmm...well...I think maybe you are right, but it's okay. I know exactly what he is. I have been searching for him." Father Bishop's smile widened and... "Wait," Chris thought, "Did his teeth look bigger?"

The subtle changes caught up in Chris' mind and he looked closer at the priest. It was in that moment that Chris caught a glimpse and saw beyond the façade of what Father Bishop really was. It scared Chris and he jumped back in his seat. He looked at the priest like he had never seen him before. This was true–he had never seen him in this light before.

Father Bishop's smile widened. "It's okay, Chris, but I do feel that I must tell you something. I'm not really a priest."

Chapter Twenty-Four

Chris stumbled out of the pew, not taking his eyes off of Father Bishop. The priest followed right behind him. "What are you?" Chris asked.

"I guess I'm kind of like Ol' Ned, except different," he replied.

"Are..." Chris started, but lost his voice and had to start again. "Are you going to do something to me?"

The "thing" that had been Father Bishop stopped and looked at Chris "Heavens no, Chris. I've been compelled to come here and put a stop to all of this. You see, there is much more at stake here than just your memories or the timeline of your life."

Chris stopped and waited for more of an explanation. Father Bishop continued, "I didn't know who it was, though I knew something was going on here in this little village."

"But people tell you all sorts of things as a priest, don't they?" Chris asked.

"Yes. Yes, they do, but if they don't remember changes, then they can't tell me about them. You are the first person that happened to remember and finally put the last piece together."

"What's going on here? What exactly are you and

Ol 'Ned?" Chris asked. By this time, he had gained control over his fear because Father Bishop had not made any threatening moves so far.

"It's going to be hard to explain, so pay attention. I guess we are beings that can travel different realms...and see or interact with the threads of life..."

"What?" Chris interrupted. "Realms?"

"Think of it like this...See that rug there?" The thing that was Father Bishop pointed to a rug near the front door.

"Yes."

"Well, think of that rug and every single thread in it, as a life, or an entity–everything from a microorganism to a great blue whale."

"Okay."

"Now imagine that other, similar rugs–with a thread shifted here or there, or different threads altogether–are stacked upon one another." Father Bishop stopped long enough to see if this explanation was connecting with Chris, before continuing. "Then you have something that comes along–in this case, something like Ol' Ned–that burns out a thread. What happens next is, now that the thread has been removed, there can't be two rugs exactly the same, so they combine as one. When that happens, a large amount of energy is expended and that's why you see these strange storms happen–like the one you are seeing now. Two different worlds, or timelines, are converging."

"Why do I remember things when others don't?"

Chris asked.

"You know how things close to a fire get charred?"

"Yes."

"Same thing happens to the threads surrounding the one thread that's burned out of existence. They char…and those closest are disrupted and can't remember. But with the threads that aren't as close, it takes time for those memories to change. That's one of the reasons people remember something a certain way, like an event, and when they go look it up, they find out it didn't occur like they had remembered. Of course, sometimes it's just due to a faulty memory, but sometimes, it was a correct memory that had changed because of one of these threads being burned out."

It took a moment for Chris to wrap his head around all of it. The being continued, "And so I see all the rugs, even now, and sometimes it's hard to pick out the areas of individual threads being removed, or which two rugs are converging. We just know that something strange is happening in a certain area, on a certain rug, and show up. Sometimes, it's quick. Other times, it can take years to track down the disruption. I've been waiting here three years, so far, but I've been other places far longer."

Chris felt relieved but it was so abstract that he thought his mind felt three times the size it should be, trying to understand the concept. "It's okay, Chris. If we can fix this, it will all work out. You see, this Ol' Ned–he eats things out of existence. It gives him power. It's one thing to eat a lesser being but quite another to eat a sentient. It's a delicacy, and sometimes, you have rogue entities such as this hermit of yours, that develop a taste for it and take things too far. I'm here to fix things if I can, because if I don't and one too many threads is removed...well, it all falls apart."

"So, we can fix this?" Chris asked, hopefully.

"It's possible. Everything is a thread. It just depends on what happens."

At this point, Chris didn't care. All he heard was "fixing things" and that gave him hope that maybe things would turn out okay and he'd see his brother again. The storm continued to rage outside.

"So, would you be willing to show me the way?"

"You mean now? The storm..." Chris began.

"The longer we wait, the harder it's going to be for things to return to normal...well... normal as you would know it to be."

Chris didn't really care about the storm, but he brought it up, thinking that this being who called itself Father Bishop, wouldn't want to be out in it...but what did he know? He had no idea what it would or wouldn't want to do. "I'm ready," Chris said.

"Great. Show me the way."

"One thing before we go–what's your real name?" Chris asked.

The question caught the being off guard. "I am called...well...you can just continue to call me

Bishop. I would tell you my full name, but you wouldn't be able to pronounce it. There is a part of it that sounds like 'Bishop,'" he said, then chuckled as he explained some more. "Yeah–when I came here, I decided to go with that, but after the fact, it sounded kind of funny to me when you included the title of 'Priest' or 'Father.' Then, it just kind of stuck."

Chris nodded and they opened the door. The torrential downpour awaited them. It was cold and came down in sheets. Lightning and thunder came and went with such force that it reminded Chris of being at a rock concert with strobe lights and loudspeakers that caused his insides to shake. He was slightly afraid to get struck by lightning, but it didn't stop him. Living a life without his brother wasn't one he wanted to experience, so he stepped out into the rain with Bishop following him.

They made their way back down along road which lead out of town and to the pond, where they would turn into the woods. They met no cars, nor did they even see anyone else. Although Chris still had countless questions, they couldn't really carry on a conversation, due the storm being so loud. They would have had to shout to hear one another if they had wanted to, but since they both had goals and a destination to think about, the trek remained quiet. When they got to the pond, Bishop turned and grabbed Chris to bring him closer so he could hear.

"Whatever happens up there..." Bishop yelled. "Once we engage, something is going to happen. Either he or I will win this fight but whatever happens, you have to run immediately. It's dangerous."

Chris nodded and they were about to cross into the woods, but Bishop grabbed him again, and said "One more thing–you won't remember me after this."

Chris became alarmed. "What?" he shouted back.

Bishop looked at him seriously. "Either I erase him, or he erases me. Either way, things are going to change. Anyway, I just wanted to say 'thank you' for giving me the final piece to this puzzle. You're a nice kid. I will always remember you." He patted Chris on the back, looked him over one more time and nodded before turning toward the woods. They entered and the canopy of trees protected them, to some degree, from the rain, but they were already drenched and waterlogged. It was slow-going as they made sure of their footing as they went. It wasn't extremely steep terrain but, in the wetness, one wrong step and down the hill you'd go.

They made their way until they finally broke into the clearing where Ol' Ned had his cabin, but he was nowhere to be seen. The rain had let up now, as the storm seemed to have subsided. All the bluster was blown out of it and receded as it passed. The roar had quieted and all that was left was a light sprinkle, which didn't bother Chris, only because he was already past the point of being annoyed, being both soaked and emotionally exhausted. Besides the light falling of rain, and distant rumbles, it was quiet. Both Chris and Bishop looked around the area suspiciously. Even though Ol' Ned wasn't to be seen, his presence was still felt. Chris couldn't explain it, but he knew that Ol' Ned knew that they were there.

The silence was broken by Ol' Ned, who spoke from both nowhere and everywhere. Chris didn't know if it was in his own head or if it really came from everywhere. "So, Chris–you came back. Did you come back for some 'help?' And who is that you brought with you?"

The look on Bishop's face became grim. He stepped forward to the center of the clearing and faced the cabin. Bishop spoke and his voice boomed as it took on the same "everywhere and nowhere at once" quality that Ol' Ned had shown. "Nedistravarus–I have been searching and waiting for you to show your hand. You have eluded me for far too long. I command and compel you, by your name, to face me for judgment."

"Ah…yes…I see. You've finally come. I'm more powerful than I've ever been so yes, let's settle this," came the reply. There was no fear in the voice of Ol' Ned.

The reply did not deter the determination that Bishop displayed. His face somehow became grimmer in the anticipation of what was to come. Bishop gritted his teeth and spoke. "Show yourself, devil."

The cabin shimmered, as did the entire clearing. The whole scene wavered like a program on a TV channel that didn't quite come in all the way. The illusion shook back and forth a slow vibration until it melted away, leaving a large, gaping cave that was filled with a strange, blue light that illuminated its interior. It was vibrant, even in the daylight and in the middle of the entrance stood Ol' Ned. He wasn't a hermit; he was something sinister. He had secluded himself out here in the woods, slowly creeping into the lives of those in the community until he had control. He took lives for gain and souls for personal enhancement, no matter the cost. Chris immediately and finally understood the nature of this thing. This was the kind of entity that would sacrifice the world, or all the "worlds," as Bishop had described, for power. Chris couldn't even imagine such evil even existed until he felt what was emanating from Ol' Ned, now that he could see him in his true light.

"Well, here I am," Ol' Ned said with confidence. "I've been tired of being careful, anyway. I knew you were close but couldn't pinpoint who or where you were. Now that we've become acquainted, I plan to fully unleash my hunger on this world after I deal with you."

Bishop looked at Chris, "I think you should leave."

Ol' Ned broke in, "Oh…he should stay, because he's next."

"But I never asked for your help for anything," Chris said.

"It doesn't matter. Once I have him and his soul," Ol' Ned said, indicating Bishop, "I will no longer be caged by the rules that have held me back for so long. Then, this whole town…state…world is mine. So, sure, go ahead and run. It won't change anything. You are only delaying the inevitable."

"You are so sure of yourself," Bishop said. "You have no idea who I am…do you?"

"It doesn't matter who you are. You are a balancer, so I know what you are capable of," Ol' Ned said.

"Silence, you fool!" Bishop said as his form started to grow. "I am no balancer. I'm just like you." His teeth grew, and his eyes became glowing coals in his face, or behind the mask that was his face. The outer, apparent "shell" of the priest started to fall off the being that had been concealed behind it.

Ol' Ned hissed, and sensing what was coming, started changing forms. Maybe it had always been an illusion, but whatever it was, it didn't matter at this point. Chris could see the monster growing from behind the façade of Ol' Ned.

Bishop continued, "My name is Reordibichapinolopolich." Chris heard him say his name, but the pronunciation was not within his mind's comprehension, as was that of Ol' Ned when he heard it. His brain just filled in the blanks with sounds of his familiar, spoken language that somewhat resembled what he had just heard.

Whatever Bishop's real name was, the gravity of its meaning became apparent. The clearing suddenly became cold and dark, as if a shadow had sprung up out of nowhere. Even more impressive was that Ol' Ned's demeanor changed from one of apparent confidence to one of weariness.

"Yes, I see. You have heard of me," Bishop said.

"I have," Ol' Ned said. "You've betrayed your kind."

"No, but I do have a certain agreement and that agreement suits me with the balancers. You see, Ned, there's a certain order to things, and when it is disturbed, it needs to be brought back into alignment. The balancers have never been powerful enough for our kind and so, here I am. An anomaly? Sure...but your actions brought me here, not mine."

The forms that they took were enormous. Their faces mirrored one another except for different coloring and markings. They both towered over Chris and looked to him what he imagined dragons would look like...at least that was the closest thing his mind could attribute to what he saw. By this time, their voices boomed and echoed, not unlike rumbles of thunder, shaking the ground during their conversation.

Bishop looked down at Chris once more, and said, "It's time! Go!" Bishop then headed to take on Ol' Ned.

The sudden attention from something so large caused him to bolt immediately, his feet thinking for him. Behind him, he heard the clash of two large bodies as the battle started. The ground truly rumbled under the weight of...whatever they were. The battle raged on and he not only heard it while he made his way down the hill, but he could also feel it, like massive trees crashing in the forest, causing the ground to shake each time. By this time, the sun shone at an angle and the clouds overhead took on a new hue of strange colors that swirled. This played visual tricks with the downcast shadows of the trees. Chris had to slow down to make sure he didn't fall. It was fifteen minutes later when Chris made it to the road.

He looked back up the wooded hill. The battle seemed to have come to an end, as the thunderous rumbles had subsided, but not before one of the beings let out a final scream that reverberated in Chris' ears. There was a moment of quiet reprieve, like the world was taking a deep breath. Then all of a sudden, like the world was exhaling that deep breath, a huge explosion and shockwave erupted from the top of the hill. He could see the shockwave coming as it knocked him off his feet and caused him to fly into the air, coming to rest on his back, a few feet away.

He was worried about the outcome of what happened on the hill. Whatever had happened, it was over. He breathed heavily from all the running and high emotions of the day. The clouds overhead again darkened, with telltale signs of an upcoming storm that would likely be the kind that the residents of the area would talk about for days to come. The clouds were angry-looking, and Chris could see the lightning flash from cloud to cloud, building in brilliance and frequency. His head also started to hurt again, as the migraine–or whatever it was–was coming back. His mind was so full of memories and with another storm coming again so quickly, he knew something definitely happened on that hill. With the rapidly changing weather and his intense head pain, he knew that he better get moving. He made his way back to the farm and Aunt Christie's house, not knowing what would await him.

The clouds made the world appear as if it were night. Chris had never seen a weather event quite like this. He stumbled down the road, dealing with the pain in his head and the darkness, only seeing the road directly in front of him when the lightning flashed. The flashes were relatively frequent, which helped him find his way, but they also intensified his headache. He made the last turn into the driveway and saw the door and the warm light inside the house. It was welcoming and gave him feelings of safety and peace.

The migraine had been excruciating, but as he stepped up to the front door, it melted away. Chris took a deep breath to steady himself and turned the knob to step inside.

"Where have you been?" Brian asked, "You had us worried. You seemed to have disappeared and then the storm came. Aunt Christie and Uncle Bob were about to go out looking for you in the truck."

Chris stood stunned in the doorway, one foot inside. Brian was sitting at the kitchen table. Immediately, tears streamed down Chris' face as he rushed inside and tackled his brother in a full-body hug.

"What is wrong with you?"

"I'm...just...so...glad you're here." Chris was about to choke out, being full of emotion, then took a deep breath. "You have no idea."

The door to the kitchen from the hallway opened and Aunt Christie walked into the room as she was talking to someone behind her.

"Well, I don't know where he is, Sam. We will go look..." she said, then stopped suddenly when she saw

Chris holding Brian, weeping. "Oh! Here he is. Are you okay?"

Sam came into the room after Aunt Christie. Chris let go of Brian long enough to attack Sam with the same intense hug he had just given his brother. "And you're here too! I'm so glad!"

Sam looked at Chris like he had lost his mind. "Of course I am. Where have you been? What's wrong with you?"

"I just asked him that," Brian said.

"I'm fine," Chris managed. "It's just so good to see all of you."

The relief that Chris felt was almost indescribable. It was like being held underwater and holding your breath, then finally breaking the surface to get that first breath of fresh air. The emotions he was experiencing were deep and exhilarating. And for the first time since the summer began, which really hadn't been that long ago, Chris felt at ease and his anxiety was dissipating. He went back over to his brother and hugged him again, just to make sure.

"Stop it!" Brian protested.

"No," Chris replied. Brian gave in and waited it out, then finally asked, "You done?"

"Maybe. Ok, now I am." Chris let go and sat down at the kitchen table.

Aunt Christie was still curious. "You mind telling us what happened?"

Chris couldn't think of anything to say except,

"It's been a very long and strange day..."

Epilogue

Through the following day, the news discussed how devastating the storm that rolled through the night before had been. It was described as "the storm of the century."

While Chris still had memories of all the strange events, he checked the town the next day, with Sam and Brian in tow. Mrs. Willing was back in the store. The church hadn't been burned to the ground. Chris even found out later that Rocket, the Darlings' horse, was back. When they passed the Catholic church, it was closed and apparently had been closed for the past three years. Hmm…that was different.

New memories, just like previous times when things shifted, fought for dominance and eventually won. The old ones became like dreams upon waking, slowly fading away to the point that Chris was unsure whether they were even real. The days that followed fell back in line with normalcy.

The only downside of this new reality was that the boys never got close to the Darling girls, but Chris was okay with that, considering everything else. As time went on and as hard as Chris tried to remember everything, he had forgotten most of it by the end of summer. He took down notes but even that didn't help after a while. He began to wonder if he was writing notes for a story or something. Eventually, he lost interest and didn't keep up with it anymore. They fell back into the same routine as previous summers: going to church, hanging out at the farm and going into the larger, nearby towns every once in a while, to visit other family members.

Every time he saw Jessica and Erin, though, it felt oddly like he had something just on the tip of his tongue or tip of his memory that he just couldn't put together. No matter what he did, it just didn't connect, and he couldn't shake the feeling. He guessed that it could have just been him feeling awkward around girls. He didn't know for sure.

One Friday, at the beginning of August a few weeks later, Chris and Brian's mom returned to pick them up and head home to Florida. She stayed the weekend and they left Sunday morning to drive back.

"So, boys...how was your summer?" she asked.

"Nothing ever happens here," Brian said.

"Yeah. It was kind of boring," Chris said.

"Oh, come on. It couldn't have been that bad," their mom said.

"It was like it always is. It wasn't bad; it wasn't great; it just was. Brian was right– nothing ever happens here. The only good thing is that I get to see family like Aunt Christie, Uncle Bob and Sam. That, and the food is pretty fantastic," Chris replied. "But I'm looking forward to getting back home."

And with that, Chris settled into the front seat, while Brian sat in the back for the long ride home to

Florida. Chris couldn't help but to think of his friend Mike, who had invited him to come hang out at the pool if he had stayed in Florida for the summer. He imagined all the adventures they could have had, had he just stayed home. He was certain that his friend probably had a better and more adventurous summer than he did...in good ol' southern Illinois.

About the Author

J.E. Jack can be found reading everything from historical textbooks to young adult mystery/thrillers. Developing a love for adventure and self-learning early in life, Joshua has traveled the world and been fortunate enough to survive. With almost two decades of involvement in the military/law enforcement community, he tries to bring different experiences, emotions, and thoughts to his readers. "The Hermit" is his second novel and he is now working on the next writing project. He currently lives near the coast of Louisiana with his family.

If you enjoyed the book and want see future books by this author, be sure to join us on facebook.com/authorJEJack.

Or…feel free to send him an email at authorjejack@gmail.com.

Review the Book

You've read my book. Thank you so much! I truly hope you have enjoyed the journey. Your feedback is really important to me so if you have a moment, please tell me what you liked about it.

You can leave a review, as well as find my other works by visiting the following: amazon.com/author/jejack.

Made in the USA
Columbia, SC
13 September 2021

45413150R00171